The Florentine Table

THE
FLORENTINE
TABLE

Paul Durst

CHARLES SCRIBNER'S SONS
New York

Copyright © 1980 Paul Durst

Library of Congress Cataloging in Publication Data

Durst, Paul.
    The Florentine table.

    I. Title.
PZ.D967Fl [PS3554.U695]   813'.54   80-14779
ISBN 0-684-16526-0

1 3 5 7 9 11 13 15 17 19   F/C   20 18 16 14 12 10 8 6 4 2

Printed in the United States of America.

FOR
Robin, Bruno, David, and Ruth

I

I DREAMED LAST NIGHT THAT I WAS BACK AGAIN IN Bentley Square, walking alone by the moonlight. Footsteps silent, as they are in dreams, I crossed the pavement where sharp leaf shadows lay underfoot beneath the trees and stood once more before the house. Tall and white it rose, between its neighbors on either side, mellowed elegance, serene, its Georgian façade silvered with soft August moonlight.

There was no hint of terror.

In the dream I saw the To Let sign in the window, just as it had been when I had gone back to London, briefly, alone, to collect the things Liz no longer had the heart to face. There had been no takers then, not even for what was described as a "desirable property in an exclusive neighborhood." But the story would die and be forgotten and in a few months someone else would come along who either didn't know or didn't care what had happened there. A nine days' wonder. People have short memories.

As I turned away in my dream I thought I heard a stifled cry from somewhere inside and it made my blood run cold. I paused to look back but it did not come again. The square and the house and the city were silent. But as I walked away I saw the shadow on the pavement beside me, clear-etched by moonlight, keeping step. Even as I looked I knew there would be no one there, only the shadow moving next to my own.

The cry came again and I slid out of the dream into wakefulness. On the pillow beside me Liz stirred and whimpered, her feet making jerky motions as a dog does when it is said to be dreaming of chasing rabbits.

I touched her shoulder. Gently.

"Liz?"

She opened her eyes and for a moment I saw the terror before it faded and she knew I was there. "Oh, God, Ray!" she cried, and snuggled against me. The cry was half anguish, half relief at being released from her own nightmare. "Will it ever stop?"

"It will," I said and kissed her cheek. "It just takes time to forget, that's all." But for a long time after her breathing became deep and regular again I lay staring into the darkness, wondering if we could ever forget.

Since the day we were married, Liz and I had talked and dreamed of living in London. As some young couples dream of escaping to an island in the South Pacific, we dreamed of London. Just why it should be London was something of a mystery. Neither of us had any relatives in England and we loathed big cities. Liz was born in a small town in Massachusetts and I came from a village in the Lackawanna Valley of Pennsylvania. When we married neither of us had been anyplace bigger than Boston or Scranton. We spent our honeymoon in New York and hated the place. Yet for some reason we seemed inexorably drawn toward London even then. One day, we promised ourselves, we would go there. We would save our money until we had enough to spend just one year in London. We would rent a small Georgian house off some quiet square, yet near enough to the center of things to be able to see and do all that we had dreamed of.

The chance, when it finally came, was unexpected. We had all but forgotten our dream, settled as we were into the pleasantly humdrum life of a university town. I was now a professor of English lit, struggling to find time to write. We had been married nearly fourteen years and had two sons—Edward, twelve, and Richard, ten. Liz had gotten into TV and movie script writing and, after modest successes, had finally sold a script called *Who Killed Candy Jones?* to a big Hollywood producer. And, to my surprise, my new novel, *Gray Dawn in Arcady*, had started out halfway up the best-seller list and had stayed there long enough to more or less establish the name of Ray Armacost.

My publisher was delighted, and that spring invited us to his country place in the Adirondacks. It was there that he asked me if I would like to do a series of novels on English historical subjects. He would give me a big advance if I would be willing to go to London to do extensive research. Would I be interested?

It was one of those questions that seems too good to be true. Here was our chance for maybe a year or more in London, our dream about to become a reality. The only problem might be that the boys would hate to leave their school and their friends. I had ready in my head a whole list of arguments about the fun and educational value of travel when I broke the news to Edward and Richard that afternoon. But I didn't need to convince them. They listened to my announcement, shrugged, and then Eddie asked Liz if he could have a Coke.

"Not before your dinner," Liz said automatically, a bit deflated that our longtime dream of London made so little impression on the younger generation. "Aren't you excited?"

"No," Eddie said blandly. "We figured you'd go there someday."

Later that night we lay making plans and listening to the wind sighing through the pines.

"I thought the boys took the news very well," I said. "Almost blasé."

"Do you think they took it *too* much for granted, Ray? The way Edward said 'We figured you'd go there someday'—as if he had already known. Before we did. It's—well, almost uncanny."

"They probably had heard us talking about it."

"But when we talked about it, Ray, it's been at times like this. When we're alone."

"Honey, you're making too much of it." She lay still then but I could tell that she was awake. For a long time.

"Ray, I'm scared."

"You're just nervous because we're moving into a new situation. Like waiting to go into the church to get married."

"No, that's a different kind of scared. That's pleasant. This isn't. I can't explain it."

That had a sobering effect. Perhaps it was the power of suggestion. Or perhaps it is simply that when something you've wanted a long time finally is about to happen it loses some of its flavor. Whatever it was, I began to feel it too.

We said nothing more after that. But it was a long time before either of us went to sleep.

"Dad, will you buy that table?"

We were in the Portobello Road. It was Tuesday morning in July, sunny and warm. Warm for England, that is. We were shopping for knickknacks, small *objets d'art* to fill the vacant niches and wall spaces in the house we'd found in Bentley Square.

The house was a stroke of luck. If we had ordered it built to wait for us for two hundred years, it couldn't have been more perfect. And, as the rental agent said, to find such a place empty in the heart of London and be able to move in without waiting was unbelievable.

Well, almost without waiting. It was unfurnished. Which meant we had to live in a hotel until we'd at least gotten some beds in and a table to eat off of. The rent was something else. Even for London it was pretty steep. Which may have had something to do with its being empty. But we had waited fourteen years for this and money was no longer a real problem. Besides the very generous advance from my publisher, Liz had come armed with introductions to some American film producers and directors who were working at various London studios. Already she had landed a script to rewrite, so she would be busy doing work she loved and would make money too. There would be plenty of ways to spend it.

To furnish a Georgian house in Georgian style costs a lot, we discovered. We soon learned, too, that an American accent is quite often a definite drawback when buying antiques. There are some dealers who believe that every American has a personal account at Fort Knox.

So on this morning in Portobello Road we were searching among the stalls and barrows for the odds and ends, the hoped-for "treasure" among the junk. Something as big as a table, for a house now adequately furnished, was not part of the plan. Particularly not the one to which Richard and Edward were calling our attention.

Liz turned to look. "My God, how awful!" was her immediate reaction. I saw the hurt expression on the boys' faces and felt a tinge of annoyance at her for hurting their feelings.

"We'll buy it with our savings," Edward said in an injured tone. "It could go in one of our rooms. You wouldn't have to look at it, Mom."

I couldn't see it clearly from where I was standing so I pushed my way through the crowd around the stall and came up beside Liz and the boys. My taste in furniture is not as sophisticated as Liz's but even I could see that this was too ornate for a Georgian interior. It looked Italian, with a semicircular marble top resting on a confusion of carved gesso and gilt. The heavy curved legs ended in feathered clawlike feet clutching gilt orbs the size of croquet balls. It was altogether too rococo to fit in with our other things, but in the proper surroundings it wouldn't have been bad. I couldn't see that it justified Liz's outburst. Then for the first time I saw what she was looking at and some warmth went out of the sunshine.

At the top of each of the front legs and joining them to the decorated frieze were two—well, *faces*. Normally they would have been cherubs, but there was nothing cherubic about these. The artisan who had carved them may have intended them as a joke, but it was a joke that had backfired. They were more gargoyle than human, yet there was enough humanity in them to make them pitiful. Like damned souls trapped forever between heaven and hell. Any feeling of pity they engendered was immediately dispersed by the malevolence with which these things looked back at you. As though they hated all humankind and were awaiting their chance.

I looked at Liz. Her eyes were pleading with me, her lips trembling. "Please don't buy it for them," she whispered. "I couldn't live with those things around."

The Cockney stall holder bustled up, spotting a sale. "Nice table, guv. Genuine Eyetalian antique. Fetch a thousand dollars back in New York, that would." He had heard the American accent.

Eyes on me. Liz's. The boys'. The stall holder's. And *those* things'.

"How much?" I found myself asking and not knowing why.

Liz said, "Please, Ray!"

"To you, twenty quid. Delivered. And that's a steal, believe me, guv. You know what you'd pay for that in an antique shop? A hundred guineas."

I hate being fast-talked. "Then why don't you sell it to an antique dealer?" I asked, nettled.

He shrugged. "I make my money on quick turnover. Can't be bothered."

"Please, Dad," Edward coaxed. "Richard and I can pay for it. We'll keep it upstairs."

"NO!" Liz almost shouted it. The babble of nearby voices stopped. People turned to look. Even I felt embarrassed.

"Well, let's don't fall out over a goddamn table," I said, more sharply than I intended. I started to walk away and Liz and the boys followed. People tittered. I felt a little ashamed.

We went from there to the British Museum but it was a flop. I tried to pretend nothing had happened but Liz dragged around in stony silence, giving me that "you-didn't-have-to-act-like-*that*" look whenever I attempted a feeble sally to raise our spirits. The boys followed with that air of boredom only boys are capable of, and which is guaranteed to put the kiss of death on the liveliest family outing. I was determined to see it through, but by the time we'd finished the Egyptian Room even I couldn't take any more of this persecution.

I suggested lunch but nobody seemed interested. The boys said they'd rather go home and fix themselves a sandwich, and Liz had some shopping to do. Since I was already at the museum, I decided to apply for a ticket to the Reading Room and the Manuscript Room. Now that we were more or less settled, there was no point in postponing my research any longer.

We were about to go our separate ways when I overheard the boys asking Liz for taxi fare. I blew my top. "We're not *that* well off. If you're going to spend a year in this town you might as well learn to find your way around on the subway."

"Underground," Edward said.

"What?"

"They call it the underground here."

"Whatever they call it, it's a damn sight cheaper than taxis."

"They might get lost," Liz chided me. "Didn't you think of that?"

"Oh, Mom—we're not babies," Edward said with a dramatic sigh. "Russell Square to Holborn, change to the Central Line and get off at Bond Street and we're only about four blocks from home."

I was taken aback. So was Liz. "How did you know all that?"

He held up a little card covered with colored lines like a chart of the human circulatory system. "A map of the London underground system."

"Well, just be careful," I said, annoyance giving way to fatherly pride. "And if you should get lost, ask a cop."

"Bobby," Richard corrected seriously.

"Okay—bobby, then." I had to smile. It melted some of the ice.

The boys hurried off, happy in their own confidence, free of adult restraint.

Liz lingered a moment.

I took her elbow. "I'm sorry," I said, and meant it.

She smiled. "Let's just forget about that damn table—as if it never happened?"

"Sure."

"Ray, I've just thought of something. It's Wednesday and there's a matinee of *The Crucifer of Blood* at the Haymarket. You said you'd like to see it."

"It beats working," I confessed, grinning.

"I thought you'd say that. But—there's a catch."

"Oh?"

"We'll have to take a taxi or we'll miss the first curtain."

We took a taxi home from Haymarket, too.

"Ray?"

We were just turning off Piccadilly into Berkeley Street.

"Do you think it's a good idea to let the boys see us coming home in a taxi—after that lecture, I mean?"

I told the driver to stop a hundred yards short of Bentley Square and we got out and walked the rest of the way. The sun was slanting low in the west. We could see our house through the trees across the square. It looked magnificent in the sunset glow. The hum of London traffic seemed far away. Birds were actually singing in the trees.

She hung on my arm, not hurrying. It was a pleasant evening. Warm. It felt good to be alive. Especially good with the feeling that comes with having made up after a spat.

"What would you like for dinner?" she mused.

"Tell you what. Let's go out. Make it up to the boys for not getting their table. Only don't let them *know* that's the reason or they'll think they've got us under control. But I feel it's a night to celebrate."

"I do too," Liz said happily, giving my arm a squeeze. Then: "But what are we celebrating?"

"Not having bought that goddamn table!"

We laughed and felt better. From now on "the table" would be a story to retell at cocktail parties. *"We saw this table in Portobello Road. It damn near broke up our marriage. Liz didn't want me to buy it, and I didn't want to buy it, but the boys . . ."*

I opened the front door with my key. Liz went in first and I picked up the mail that was lying on the mat and glanced through it. She was taking off her coat when I heard her gasp. Liz looked horrified. I turned to see what she was looking at. And there it was. The table.

It had flowers on it. And a card addressed to Liz. I read it over her shoulder:

Dear Mom,

We know it's still a month till your birthday, but you know how you always say that it's the thought that counts and that if you see something that somebody might like you ought to get it and put it away until the time comes. Only this was too big to hide. We know you and Dad thought it was too expensive, but honest, Richard and I have been saving up for a real nice birthday present for you for a long time, so I hope you don't mind if we surprise you like this. Happy Birthday (in advance).

Your loving sons,
Edward and Richard

Liz looked up from the card. "But they *knew* I didn't like it! They heard me say . . ." She stopped and turned around to look at the table.

I shrugged. "I guess they just thought you meant it was too expensive." She glanced at the card again and went all soft and wet around the eyes.

I took a closer look at the table. "Hey, look at this, Liz! This isn't the same table."

"Of course it is. It's got the same . . ." She leaned closer. It was getting dark outside and the light in the hall was not too good. I switched on the lights. "You're right, Ray. It is a different table. Those awful faces . . . They're gone. These are positively angelic! I wonder where they found another one so like the first? Poor dears, they must have scoured London for it." She stood back. "You know darling—I think I might even begin to *like* the damn thing!"

I wasn't so sure. "Have you had a good look at those faces, Liz? Do they remind you of anybody?"

She stared a moment longer, then caught her breath. "Ray, am I seeing things?"

"I don't think so. Take away the long cherub's hair and they look like Edward and Richard a couple of years ago."

"There is a resemblance. But it's just a coincidence. It's only a resemblance." She looked at me, willing it to be so.

"Yes, I suppose I'm just worked up. Childish faces look pretty much alike, especially when they're carved on something like that. Anyway, you'd better find the boys and thank them."

A floorboard creaked on the upstairs landing and we both looked up. They were watching us, proud as new paint. Liz held out her arms to them. "Darlings! You were naughty to spend all your money."

They came tumbling down like puppies. "Do you like it, Mom? It's not too big for the hall, is it?"

"It's lovely," Liz gushed. "And the flowers, too."

"The lady next door gave us the flowers," Richard confessed. "She saw the man helping us with the table and when we told her it was a surprise for your birthday she said it would be nice to have some flowers to put on it, so she took us to her garden and picked them."

"How sweet of her. I'll have to thank her tomorrow. Now go get cleaned up. Daddy's taking us all out to dinner to celebrate."

"You're not angry, Dad—about the table?" Edward asked.

"Of course not. Only I'm surprised you found one almost exactly like the one we saw this morning."

The boys exchanged a puzzled look, glanced at the table, then at me. "It *is* the same one," they said in unison.

"But the other had . . ." Liz began, then stopped. She looked at me for support.

"Uh—different faces," I said, trying to be diplomatic. "Not as nice as these."

Edward shrugged. "It's the same table. I don't see anything different. Mom, do we have to wash again? We washed this morning."

"It wouldn't hurt. And comb your hair, too, both of you."

They went unenthusiastically up the stairs. Liz and I looked at the table without saying anything until we heard the bathroom door close and water running. Then our eyes met. "Is it?" she asked.

I frowned. "It could have been a trick of light. It was in the shadow."

She looked at it thoughtfully for a moment. "It doesn't look too bad here in the hall, does it? At least there's nothing here to clash with it."

"It ought to have a mirror hung above it."

"We'll look for one. Funny, I didn't notice how empty the hall looked before. Yes, I think I'll learn to like it. But when I saw it this morning . . . Those faces . . ." She shivered.

"I wonder if it is an antique?" I gave it a closer look. "It's old anyway. But it could be a reproduction."

"It couldn't be terribly old or he wouldn't have let it go so cheap," Liz said. "Unless we got a bargain."

The next day I went to the Public Record Office in Chancery Lane to arrange for a reader's ticket, then walked over to Foyle's bookshop in Charing Cross Road where I browsed for a while and bought a couple of books, then on to Great Russell Street where I had lunch in a little Italian restaurant. After that I crossed over to the British Museum where I spent a couple of hours in the Print Room leafing through woodcuts of the Elizabethan period, trying to create a mood that would bring some ideas into focus for my writing.

When I got home that evening the first thing I noticed was the mirror hanging above the table in the hall. And fresh flowers. Roses this time.

Liz came in from the kitchen. "Nice," I said, indicating the mirror. "How much was it?"

"Nothing. It was a present from the lady next door. And the roses. Aren't they lovely?"

"A present?" I looked at the mirror again. Like the table, it was rococo, all gilt and cherubs and bunches of grapes. It looked expensive and I said so.

"She insisted. It was in her attic and she swore she was going to throw it out. As soon as I went over to thank her for the flowers this morning she asked me in for a cup of tea. She had already brought the mirror down and cleaned it up and was about to bring it over when I rang the bell."

"We'll have to have her over for dinner some night. What's her name?"

"Sybil Rodne, without the 'y'. She says it's a bit of personal snobbery, dropping the 'y'. Separates her from the thousands of Rodneys with 'y's. She's not a snob really. I like her. A widow I think. The motherly type. About fifty, plumpish, full of good humor. Mad on gardening— you should see her garden at the back. I almost wish we had one instead of a paved patio."

"I'm glad we haven't. All we'd need would be a garden to worry about. What's for dinner? Where're the boys?"

"Scampi. The boys are next door with Sybil. They took to her right away. I suppose she's the grandmother-they-never-had sort of thing. She said that any time we wanted to go out they could come over to her or she'd come here and baby-sit. If you can call it that at their age. She even offered to have them for a week or two if we ever wanted to take a trip. When she gets back, that is. She's leaving for a month's vacation herself tomorrow. France, I think she said."

I was impressed. "Who said the English were stuffy? I'd better go next door and get the boys and thank Mrs. Rodne."

"Ray, something else she said—the table. She thinks it's genuine."

"And what does that mean?"

"A real antique. Early Italian Renaissance, fifteenth century. She says we really got a bargain. The man probably didn't know what he had. She said it's worth hundreds of pounds, maybe more."

I looked at the table with new respect.

I went next door and was about to ring the bell when the door opened and there stood a man dressed like a priest. About forty-five, distinguished, almost white hair. Maybe Liz had got it wrong. This Mrs. Rodne must be a minister's wife.

"Mr. Rodne?" I asked.

He laughed. "No, I'm afraid the trend toward matrimony favored by some of the more liberal Catholic clergy hasn't yet reached my age bracket. I'm Father George Bunting. I was just paying a social call."

"Oh. I'm Ray Armacost. We've just moved in next door. I've come to get my two boys."

He shook hands. "Your youngsters are somewhere out back. Charming lads. Intelligent, too. They seem immersed in botany at the moment. Mrs. Rodne's quite keen on it."

"So I understand. But my kids don't know a dandelion from an orchid so I'd better go to the rescue before they do some damage."

He laughed. "I'm sure Mrs. Rodne can handle them. Just go on through," he told me as he went out of the house and down the steps.

I nodded and turned inside, heading in the direction of voices from somewhere out back, picking my way through an assortment of hatcases and suitcases packed for travel. The house itself, like ours, was Georgian, built sometime in the early eighteenth century. But the Georgian elegance had been swept away by the worst possible Victorian vandalism. The basic proportions of the house outside were similar to ours, but inside it was a different story. Gloom reigned supreme. Heavy plum-colored flocked wallpaper absorbed what little light got past the chocolate-covered velvet draperies hiding the windows. Plants were every-where, proof that photosynthesis can flourish in a crack of light in a cave. Knickknacks galore filled every inch of table, floor, and wall space. Bronze horses reared, drawing bronze chariots occupied by bronze warriors. Walnut-framed horsehair chairs and sofas rigidly defied would-be sitters. Tables crouched beneath bobbed velvet coverings. And over all a smell of mold and damp mingled with the sickly sweet aroma of herbs and flowers. I found it over-whelming.

As I passed the kitchen I sneaked a quick look at the an-tique gas stove, scrubbed pine table with oilcloth covering, and painted linoleum with worn spots. The smell of last week's roast mutton seemed to cling to the walls.

"Oh, there you are, Mr. Armacost!"

I jumped guiltily as she came toward me from the glassed-in conservatory just beyond the back door. She was as Liz had said: plump, fiftyish, not unpretty. I had expected after seeing the house to find her in jet beads, bustled taffeta, and a bun hairdo. Instead she was the replica of any other well-dressed Mayfair matron. Her genuine warmth of welcome swept away the gloom.

"Mrs. Rodne?"

She took my hand. Hers was warm, plump, slightly moist. "Call me Sybil. How nice to see you! Do come through. The boys are looking over my hothouse garden."

I followed her saying, "I want to thank you for the mirror. It fits right in with the table."

"Oh, don't mention it, dear boy. I was glad to be rid of it."

We rounded the corner of the small hothouse and found Eddie and Richard with their noses pressed against a glass panel.

"Look, Dad," Richard said.

I looked. Behind the glass was the most vile-looking plant I have ever seen. Leaves a noxious dark green that gave the impression it would kill you to touch them. But the most evil-looking part of all was its flowers. Almost black, velvety—like the lining of a hearse.

"Isn't it lovely?" Sybil was saying. "It's a true *Helleborus niger*, the original 'black hellebore' known to the Greeks. The common *niger*, the 'Christmas rose,' so-called, has a white flower and is really a sport, a throwback. It took me years to propagate back to its original black state."

I couldn't bring myself to admire it but I had to say something. "What's a Christmas rose doing blooming in July?"

"Coddling does it. This blooms all the year round now."

Thank God there were other flowers that I *could* admire

before we took leave of Sybil, wishing her good weather on her vacation. On the way to our front door Eddie said, "Gee, that black flower was really something, wasn't it, Dad? Do you think Mom would like one for Christmas? I'll bet Mrs. Rodne would let us have one."

Somehow I didn't feel that Liz would appreciate it any more than I would. "I think we ought to skip it, son. Potted flowers take a lot of attention and your mother doesn't really have time. If she forgot to water the thing and it died, Mrs. Rodne would feel hurt."

Liz was frying bacon for breakfast the next morning and I was yawning and stirring a cup of instant coffee when the boys came in all excited.

"Mom, look!" they chorused.

I couldn't believe my eyes. It was a black hellebore in a small pot. Liz made a face. "It looks like a tarantula. What is it?"

"A black hellebore!" Eddie cried enthusiastically. "Look, here's a note addressed to you."

Liz took the note and read it aloud:

> Dear Liz,
>   Your menfolk were so taken with my little pet that I thought you might like a cutting for yourself. See you in a month.
>
> Love,
> Sybil

Eddie handed her the pot, glowing. Liz took it gingerly. "How nice."

The boys went upstairs to dress. Liz looked at me across the top of the ugly black flower. "What the hell will I do with it?"

I shook open the paper. "Forget to water it. With any luck it'll be dead and forgotten before she gets back."

2

We had arrived in London in mid-June and spent the next four weeks furnishing the house and settling in. The boys had bought the table for Liz in mid-July. It was a glorious summer, the first they'd had in England in three years, the local people told us. Following the advice of friends, we decided to see some of the English countryside while the weather was warm and sunny. Two days after the table arrived I bought a car, an English Ford Cortina, and we began taking short trips.

At first we behaved very much like American tourists and stuck to the well-worn trail: Oxford, Stratford-on-Avon, Broadway, Stonehenge; and the rounds of the stately homes: Woburn Abbey, Longleat—where the lions and other jungle animals looked as phony in their English setting as anything Disneyland could conjure up. We even journeyed up through the Midlands to The Dukeries and Chatsworth.

But the real enjoyment came when we grew more venturesome and began to wander on our own, following wherever our fancy led us. We found quaint little villages tucked away in unexpected places, open expanses of downland with not a soul in sight for miles, windswept moors as wild and forbidding as anything on the edge of the American West. And we loved it. Every minute of it. And whenever we encountered a party of American tourists traveling *en masse* we went the other way. There is something embarrassing about meeting hordes of your own countrymen in a foreign land, especially when the beauty and antiquity fade before uninvited lectures on comparative plumbing or the lack of hominy grits for breakfast. Just as deadly, we found, is the solitary Instant Anglophile who thinks everything English is too cute for words. There is a snake in every Eden.

But the fun had to stop sometime. The chief reptile in the boys' own carefree paradise was that old bogey, school. And, sooner or later, I had to bend my nose to the grindstone and start writing. My publisher's London counterpart, by pulling a few strings, got me a tentative interview with the headmaster of a school less than four blocks from home where the boys might be accepted as day pupils. Liz, meanwhile, had signed the contract for the film script.

One morning she took the car and the boys and drove out to Elstree Studios for a meeting with the producer. I took the underground to Russell Square and walked to the

British Museum. In the Manuscript Room, where the price-less ancient documents are kept, I checked the catalogue for several I wanted, put in request slips, then went down to the coffee room to wait while they were searched for in the archives.

As I got in line in the coffee room, something about the man in front of me seemed vaguely familiar. When it came his turn to pay he turned toward me and smiled suddenly in recognition.

"Mr. Armacost! What a pleasant surprise. Come and join me—if we can find a table." It was the priest, Father Bunting. We were eventually forced to share a table with a pair of university students who smelled as though they hadn't bathed for a month. They huddled in morose silence, apparently eavesdropping on our conversation and glaring at Father Bunting's dog collar. Every time they heard my American accent they exchanged glances as though trying to decide whether or not to start an anti-nuclear demonstration then and there. When they finally left, kicking the leg of the table and spilling my coffee—maybe it *was* an accident—Father Bunting chuckled.

"You're extremely susceptible to an aura of hostility, aren't you?" he said.

I hadn't meant for it to show. "It wasn't so much the aura as the aroma that I objected to," I said, trying to laugh it off.

"Yes, there's something in the old saying about cleanliness and godliness. But I was interested in your reaction. You're sensitive, that's obvious. But then I imagine most writers are. Yet yours seems to go a bit deeper."

"No, I don't think so. I'm afraid I'm depressingly normal," I said.

He seemed genuinely disappointed. "What a pity. You

see, I've read your *Gray Dawn in Arcady*, and I was impressed by one of your characters, Margot Nonsuch. She seemed to be obsessed by the existence of certain supernormal forces—call them forces of evil, if you will."

"I didn't see her that way when I wrote her." I laughed. "To me she was just a mixed-up suburban housewife who cracked under the strain of the rat race. I'm afraid you must have been reading between the lines, Father."

He looked thoughtful. "Perhaps I was. But I wonder if any of us really realizes his own potential for good or evil? Or is even aware of how delicate is the balance that can be tipped one way or the other without our being able to do anything about it."

He looked at his watch. "Sorry I got carried away."

"Not at all. Maybe we can talk about it more some other time. Over dinner perhaps. At our place. We'd love to have you and Mrs. Rodne."

"Dear Sybil." He laughed. "Yes, that would be delightful. Any time you say, Mr. Armacost."

We started up the stairs to the ground floor of the museum. "Please call me Ray. 'Mr. Armacost' sounds so formal."

"Ray it is. Are you doing some work here?"

I told him about my research, briefly. "What about yourself?"

"Oh, I'm always digging into obscure tomes and manuscripts. I do a bit of writing myself. Not in your class, of course. Mostly rather obtuse treatises on some aspect of theology. All very dull, I'm afraid."

He was going into the Reading Room. We shook hands and I renewed the invitation to dinner, promising to make a date as soon as I knew Liz's schedule. As I walked back between the display cases toward the Manuscript Room I had the feeling that Father Bunting would make very good material for a character in a novel.

Liz was bubbling over with excitement when I got home. "Guess what? Your sons have a chance at a television acting career."

"You're joking!"

"They've been offered a contract to do a series of ten commercials for a fertilizer firm. Charles Sealey—he's the director I'm rewriting this film script for—was showing us around the studio and we cut across one of the sound stages where they were doing commercials. Charles stopped to introduce us to the producer, a fellow named Leonard Harding. As soon as he saw the boys he said that they were just what he was looking for. Clean, fresh, English country types."

"Didn't he know they're a couple of bloody Yanks?"

"Sure, but they *look* as if they belong in an English country garden. They don't have to say any lines. Just be around to do things. You know, like cutting a flower and admiring it. Or helping their 'mother' pick roses, that sort of thing. The soft sell comes in voice-over. 'You, too, can grow the biggest goddamn aspidistras in the land if you use Smedley's ersatz horse manure.' "

I poured us each a drink and took a sip as I sat down to think this one over.

"You don't look happy about it," Liz said.

"Liz, do you think it's a good thing? Getting the kids stagestruck at their age?"

She draped herself in my lap and ran her fingers through my hair—something that always annoys the hell out of me but she somehow got the idea way back that I like it and now I haven't got the heart to disillusion her.

"Don't be a spoilsport, Ray. It's not as though they got the lead in a big production. That might go to their heads. But a couple of lousy little TV commercials?"

"No, I'm serious, Liz. An acting career is one thing. *If* they're talented, dedicated, and *if* they want to make it their life. But a couple of one-timers on the boob tube could have all the disadvantages of cheap notoriety and none of the advantages of a genuine acting career. How did they take it?"

She flung her arms in the air and stood up. "Blasé as could be. Not a bit impressed. They actually seemed pretty bored about the whole thing. Honestly, Ray, I think you're exaggerating."

Maybe I was. I thought it over, sipping my drink. "How soon do you have to let this TV character know about the contract?"

"I said I'd talk it over with you."

I stood up. "Well, give me a day or two to think it over."

"Ray, he wants them on the set tomorrow at nine."

"So I haven't got a day or two to think it over."

"No, not really."

"Where are the boys?"

"In Edward's room, reading I think."

"Let me talk to them."

She gave me a kiss. "Well, it's not a life-and-death matter either way."

She went back to the kitchen and I went upstairs and knocked. Edward was sprawled on his bed, facedown, reading from a book open on the floor. Richard was curled up in a chair with another book. They said "Hi, Dad," without looking up.

"What's this I hear about you two becoming big television stars? Eddie?"

"Aw, I think it's kind of stupid."

"Yeah, me, too," Richard mumbled. "Handing people plastic flowers and grinning silly grins."

"But don't you think it would give you a bit of prestige when you go to school? All the other kids seeing you on TV?"

"Heck, no," Edward said. "They might think we're sissies or something. But they won't even see us, anyway. Kids don't watch commercials about fertilizers."

"Then you don't want to do it?"

Edward looked up and made a grimace. "Aw, I suppose we'll have to or Mom will be disappointed. She made an awful fuss about it, like it was really somethin'."

I started to leave, feeling much better. "What's this you're reading?"

"Oh, a couple of books Sybil gave us."

"Mrs. Rodne," I corrected.

"Well, she said to call her Sybil."

"What are they about?"

Richard held up the book. *Rare and Exotic Plants.* I glanced at Eddie's. *Botanical Oddities Round the World.*

"I thought you said flowers were sissy."

"These are different," Edward said. "Hey, Dad, did you know there's a plant that will actually *eat* small animals?"

"Ugh! But if you two don't wash and get downstairs in five minutes I know a couple of small animals who won't eat."

I went down the stairs with a renewed feeling of confidence in the widsom of youth. I could hear steaks sizzling as I came into the kitchen. "Should I set the table?"

"It's all set." Liz turned from the stove, brushing back a strand of hair, her look quizzical. "Well?"

I grinned at her. "Roll 'em!" I said.

The next morning Liz dropped me outside the iron gates bearing a worn brass plaque that read: "St. Bartholomew's Young Gentlemen's Boarding School." She kissed me and drove off for Elstree, the boys waving briefly through the back window. I adjusted my tie and, feeling like a freshman about to meet the dean, went in to find Mr. Ormsby Henniker-Harnsworth, the headmaster. The name alone was enough to cause a stronger spirit to quail. I was about to push the bell button on the portico when it hit me. What the hell do you call a man whose last name is Henniker-Harnsworth? I should have asked Liz. She always kept up with these little niceties. I couldn't keep saying, "Yes, Mr. Henniker-Harnsworth . . . No, Mr. Henniker-Harnsworth." On the other hand I seriously doubted that we were likely to start off on an "Ormsby" and "Ray" footing. But if you are permitted to split a jawbreaker like that, I pondered, which part do you use, the front or the behind? I decided the only safe way would be to avoid direct address if at all possible.

A sad-faced flunky ushered me into the paneled Edwardian office marked "Headmaster." Mr. Ormsby Henniker-Harnsworth rose and gave me a hand that was limp, cold, and damp. He said he was pleased to see me but his manner indicated otherwise. Accustomed as I was to the directness of straight-to-the-point American conversation, it took me some time to decipher his circumlocutions. In fact it was not until he had closed the interview with another damp handshake and a not-very-convincing statement that he would "look forward to seeing my boys" when term opened, and I found myself halfway down the gravel drive toward the iron gates, that I really began to unravel the meaning behind what he had said.

St. Bartholomew's, I gathered, was the repository of the offspring of certain titled and wealthy Englishmen. Not quite up to Eton, perhaps, but leaning in that direction. I gathered also that some of the titled and wealthy gentlemen would not take kindly to having their sons tainted by association with middle-class foreigners, but since I had come so "highly recommended" the rules could be bent a little.

I stopped at a pay phone and rang Lance Mellihew, my publisher's London counterpart, to thank him for his help and to tell him the boys had been accepted.

"There, you see, I thought they would!" he said. "Money talks."

"What money?" I asked, having visions of being overcharged.

"Why, didn't you know? Old Haliburton's father is an "old boy"—an alumnus, you would say—from St. Bartholomew's. When he went out to the States and made his fortune in publishing he endowed the school in his will. Quite handsomely, I might add. Henniker-Harnsworth couldn't risk offending the Haliburtons."

"Well, I'll be damned!" I said softly.

For the rest of that week I continued to work daily at the Public Record Office, more or less learning my way around. I had a vague notion of doing a novel in the Elizabethan period and began digging among the manuscripts of the era. It was exciting to find myself actually handling letters written between Elizabeth and Essex, but when it came to trying to decipher the calligraphy of the sixteenth century, some of the thrill dissipated and it became damned hard work.

Liz was writing at home and only going to the studio once or twice a week to check with Charles Sealey. The boys went with her on those days. At other times the studio would send a car to take them and bring them home. After two weeks their TV stint was all finished. It seemed to have made no impression whatsoever.

We began giving a few dinner parties, mostly film people Liz had met since we had come to London. We also began to go out occasionally at night. Theaters, famous restaurants, places we had often heard of but never really believed we would see. At weekends we would either go sight-seeing in London itself or, if the weather was right, drive out into the country on the little jaunts we enjoyed so much together. Looking back, I think that period of our life was one of the happiest we had ever known.

We scheduled one of our parties in early September. Nothing elaborate, just a handful of people in for drinks and a good meal. Sybil had returned from her vacation in France so we asked her. Then I remembered I had let a month slip by without keeping my promise to Father Bunting to have him over. I asked Liz about it.

"Do you think it's a good idea? I mean—well, a priest and a bunch of film people?"

She was in the living room, sitting cross-legged on the floor arranging stacks of flowers Sybil had sent over specially for the party. Holding up a gladiolus for me to admire she said, "Do you mean you're afraid they might be a corrupting influence on *him*, or do you think, being a priest, he would put a damper on things?"

"Maybe a little of each."

"What's he like?"

"Seems a nice guy. Intellectual. I think he could hold his own. He's read *Gray Dawn*. We talked about it a little."

Liz stood up and put the vase of glads on a small table. "Well, then that settles it. Maybe he'll bring up the book again and you can get Charles Sealey interested and he'll buy the film rights."

"You mercenary little devil!"

So they all came. Sealey was between divorces and brought along a tart of a starlet named Adelle Charmain who was his current sleeping partner and had a bit part promised in his new film *Adulation*. Liz had finished the script and this party was partly to celebrate. To round out the numbers Liz had asked a young actor named John Dighton and partnered him with Mary Jane Coates, a pretty little Texas filly whom Sealey had brought over from Warners as his continuity girl. Liz, always on the lookout for lame dogs to help, had asked Dighton because she knew he was out of a job. He was one of the actors the boys had worked with on their TV commercials. Now Liz was hoping Sealey might cast him in *Adulation*.

They started arriving just after seven. The boys had been fed early and packed off to a double feature with strict orders to be home on the dot of eleven, and to report in when they got home and then go straight up to bed. There would be a flask of Ovaltine and sandwiches in their rooms for a bedtime snack.

The first arrival was Sybil, with more last-minute flowers. All conventional, fortunately. No weird specimens. Liz was busy in the kitchen so Sybil arranged the flowers while I inventoried the drinks.

"It was sweet of you to ask George Bunting," Sybil

remarked as she fussed with the flowers. "He's been so looking forward to coming here."

"Oh?" I said, feeling a twinge of guilt at having let it go so long.

Strangely enough he was the last to arrive, looking very preoccupied. At first I was afraid that it had been a mistake to ask him, that the crowd was not to his taste. But he soon brightened and fell into the swing of the chatter. By the time Liz announced dinner he was quite the focus, if not exactly the life, of the party.

He was talking to Sealey and Adelle Charmain, recounting something or other that had happened to him in Israel during the Six Day War. He was a marvelous raconteur but was no show-hogger and had a knack for getting the best out of even the most reluctant conversationalist. I was glad I'd invited him.

It was Sealey who nearly ruined the evening. Either he'd had too much to drink by the time we settled back in the living room for liqueurs, or else he was trying to show off in front of his tart. Whatever the reason, I could have kicked him in the teeth when he started baiting Father Bunting about film censorship.

"I suppose if you Catholics had your way you'd ban about ninety percent of modern films, eh, Father?"

The room was suddenly quiet.

Liz was sitting on the floor beside my chair. I could feel her fingers bite into my leg. "Oh, Christ, here he goes!" she muttered.

I tried my damnedest to think of a way of changing the subject without being obvious, but my brain was foam rubber.

Bunting was sitting calmly across the room, smoking a cigar. He took it in stride, smiling. "I had rather expected you to start with the Inquisition," he said, not unpleas-antly.

Everybody laughed and it broke the tension. But Sealey took it like a slap in the face.

"That's a damn good point, Father," he said angrily when the laughter had subsided. "The Inquisition and the Catholic Church did more lasting damage to mankind than anything ever put on film."

Liz dug her fingers into my leg till I winced. "Can't you shut him *up?*" she groaned out of the side of her mouth. I took her hand in self-defense and tried to think of some-thing to say but could only swallow.

Then I caught sight of Sybil's face. She was looking, not at Sealey, but at John Dighton. I have never seen so much hate, never thought it was possible for a human look to convey so much hate. Why would she feel that way about him? She turned and saw me and smiled. I tried to smile back and at the same time listened to what Father Bunting was saying.

"Damage to men's bodies, perhaps, but not to their souls. You see, it is very unfair of us to judge, with our twentieth-century sophistication, the mental processes of the lesser-educated men of the Dark Ages. Their methods, we all accept now, were horrible. But who are we to ques-tion the sincerity of their attempt to save men's souls? The Inquisition could never happen in the present day, any more than could hanging, drawing, and quartering a live human being for criminal offense. So you see, we do pro-gress."

"Well," Sealey snorted, "I'd hardly call the Church's views on sex progressive."

"Oh, Christ," Liz moaned, "he'll be starting on the god-damn pill next!"

"Nor would I accept that the film industry's view is progressive," Bunting said mildly. "I hesitate to use a trite and worn analogy, but nevertheless it is true that a decay of morality was at the root of the disaster that befell the Roman Empire. But why should we spoil an enjoyable evening by arguing? Forces of evil do exist in the world, and how we meet them is, I feel, a matter for individual conscience."

I was just breathing a sigh of relief that the matter was closed when John Dighton kicked the ball and kept it rolling. But at least he directed it toward more neutral territory.

"Do you mean that, Father? What you said about 'forces of evil'? Surely a man as educated as you doesn't really *believe* that such a thing as the Devil exists?"

"Would anybody like another drink?" Liz sang out merrily, jumping to her feet. Nobody took the slightest notice of her. They were all waiting for Father Bunting to reply. With a sigh she sank back down.

The priest looked surprised at Dighton's question. "Yes, of course. Don't you?"

Dighton laughed. "Good God, no! A Devil with horns and a tail and all that?"

"Ah, now—that is your description, not mine," Father Bunting said. "Once again you are drawing on an ancient concept to explain something that exists today. But because man has come to disbelieve in the actuality of a figure with cloven hooves and horned head does not remove *him* from existence. What I call God is to me the personification of Ultimate Good; what I call the Devil is the personification of Ultimate Evil. But I could not draw you an accurate picture of either one. Yet I know both exist."

I was astonished that Adelle Charmain had sufficient intelligence to follow the argument this far and it shook me when she opened her mouth and joined in.

"If God is so good, then why does he allow evil to exist? I mean, look what happened in Viet Nam and South Africa and places. How can he just sit up there and let things like that *happen?*"

Sealey chuckled. "Looks like the only way you're going to get out of this, padre, is to quote something like 'The wisdom of God passeth all understanding.' "

Liz hissed to me, "It's the *peace* that passeth all understanding."

I didn't know whether to get up and refill everybody's drink to try to distract them, or to skip it in case more booze might only inflame the argument. I decided to sit still.

Father Bunting continued to take it good-naturedly. "We're getting into deep theological waters. But to put it briefly, if you believe in life after death, then man's sojourn on this earth is but a flicker in eternity, and all the suffering, great though it may seem to us now—and, in many cases, *unjust* as it may seem—is infinitesimal. In short, life on earth is meant to be only a testing ground."

"But if God is all-powerful," Dighton interrupted, "why would he let the Devil set up business in opposition?"

The French carriage clock on the mantelpiece began to strike eleven. I heard the front door open, whispers—then Eddie and Richard poked their faces briefly around the door to let Liz know they were home. A second later they were making quiet noises as they went up the stairs.

Bunting's face grew very serious as he considered Dighton's question. He glanced at his watch and then looked across at Sybil. I wondered if he was looking for an excuse to go. I couldn't blame him if he was.

"The Devil," he said slowly, "is very necessary. Without evil, there could be no good."

There was a general murmur of dissent, or wonder—I'm not sure which. I thought I could glimpse a little of what he meant, but it was gone in a flash. Whatever it was I did see, I could never put into words. I only knew that I believed Bunting knew what he was talking about.

He stood up. "I'm terribly sorry, but I really must go."

Good-byes were said, good-naturedly. Liz and I saw him to the door. He thanked us and said he had enjoyed the evening very much, and sounded as though he meant it. Sybil came out with a last-minute reminder about some book she'd wanted to borrow from him and we left them talking in the hall and went back to our guests.

"He chickened out!" Sealey was muttering, helping himself to more brandy. "Once you pin them down they always chicken out."

He annoyed me. Both by his free hand with my brandy *and* his remark. After all, Bunting was our guest and was entitled to his views.

"I don't think he did," I said, sharply enough to draw a look from Liz. I knew she was thinking I was killing her chance of another script from Sealey. But I didn't give a damn, the guy was a boor. Liz didn't *have* to work. And she certainly didn't have to swallow insults from him just because he might throw a script her way.

"Of course he did. All that crap about evil being necessary for good. Jesuit double-talk!"

Sybil came back just then. I know she heard him but she just kept smiling and started talking to Mary Jane

Coates as though nothing had happened. The phone rang in the hall and Liz went to get it. Sealey started nuzzling Adelle and I wished they'd get the hell out of there and go to bed. Someplace else. I turned my back on them and talked to the others.

"John!" Liz called, beckoning Dighton. He went out and I heard him talking on the phone. A few minutes later he was back smiling.

"Good news?" I asked.

"Not bad. I've got another series of TV commercials."

"How did they know where to find you at this hour of the night?" Mary Jane asked.

Liz spoke up. "They didn't. Leonard telephoned to ask if the boys could do a retake tomorrow. Somebody accidentally erased one of the videotapes. It happened to be the one John was in with Eddie and Richard, so when Leonard said he was trying to get hold of John as well . . ." She shrugged and turned away, calling, "Coffee coming up."

"Where's the john?" Mary Jane asked.

Liz pointed down the hall and Mary Jane left. A few minutes later she was back, a strange expression on her face. "Find it?" I asked.

She gave me a curious look, as though she hadn't heard me. Then her eyes focused. "Oh! Yes, I found it." She seemed to shiver.

"You're not sick, are you?"

"No . . ." She hesitated. "I hope you don't mind my saying this, Ray, but I can't help it. That dreadful table out there in the hall. I've never seen anything so . . . well, if that priest believes in evil I think I know what he means. Those *faces!*"

(3 5)

I felt a tingle of alarm and looked for Liz but she had gone to make the coffee. I excused myself and went out into the hall. The only light came from the upstairs landing and from the room I had just left, so the table was partly in shadow. I peered close for a look at the faces. My God I got a shock. They were leering at me as they had been that first morning in Portobello Road. I was fumbling behind me for the light switch when I heard the sound of muffled laughter from one of the boys' rooms upstairs. I switched on the hall light.

The faces on the table, in the brighter light, were benign, cherubic. I switched the light off. The faces remained sweet and smiling even in the shadow. So it was just an optical illusion, a trick of the light. I went back.

"It's just the light," I told Mary Jane. "When you first look at them in the shadows they look pretty horrible, I'll admit. But have a look at them when you leave and you'll see what I mean."

The party broke up just after one o'clock. Mary Jane remembered to look at the table again. "Oh, yes, I see what you mean," she said. "It's really a kind of pretty table, isn't it?"

"What was Mary Jane saying about the table?" Liz asked a little later as we scraped the dishes and piled them on the drainboard. I started to tell her what happened, then decided against it. No point in worrying her.

"She was just admiring it, that's all," I said. I undid her apron at the back, and it fell to the floor.

"Stop it, Ray!"

"You look adorable when you're angry." I kissed her. When the kiss grew too insistent she wriggled away, laughing.

"Look—not tonight, Josephine! It's nearly two in the

morning." She hung up the apron and gave a final glance at the kitchen. "Mrs. Bloggs can tidy up in the morning. Let's go to bed. I'm tired."

"You run along," I told her. "I've got to put the drinks away. Wouldn't want to leave temptation in the path of poor old Mrs. Bloggs."

"Don't be too long, darling, or I'll be asleep and you'll wake me up and then I won't be able to get back to sleep."

"That's too complicated for me to figure out at this hour of the morning."

I heard her go upstairs while I was locking the bottles away. She stopped on the landing and the door creaked as she looked in at the boys. Then the door closed quietly and I heard her go into the bathroom and the sound of running water. I emptied the ashtrays and took them to the kitchen. I was going back to the living room for my cigarette lighter when I caught sight of the table. This time I felt something cold turn over inside me.

The faces were back. The evil ones. Leering at me. And now there was no question of light or shadow, for the hall light was on as well as the one on the upstairs landing. I closed my eyes and opened them again. They were still there. *This is impossible*, I told myself. *It's the brandy on the top of too much food.* But I knew it wasn't imagination or the brandy or anything else. I put out my hand to touch the face nearest me and I felt my fingers shaking. Suddenly I heard a god-awful scream from somewhere upstairs. Liz! She must have slipped on the bath mat and hurt herself. I bounded up the stairs two at a time, but when I reached the landing Liz came running out of the bathroom wrapping her robe about her.

"Was that you?" I asked.

"No, it sounded as if it came from Richard's room."

I ran down the hall and opened the door with Liz right behind me. The light from the hall fell across Richard's face as he lay in bed. He was moaning slightly, moving his head from side to side. Beads of sweat lay shining on his forehead. I shook him gently by the shoulders.

"Dickie?" I hadn't used that name since he was a toddler. He didn't like it, said it sounded sissy. But in moments of stress, like the time he fell off his bike and split his head, it came automatically. He was a little boy in need of help.

He opened his eyes and seemed surprised and relieved to find us there.

"Did I yell?" he asked sleepily.

I gave a little laugh of relief. "Boy, you sure did. Were you having a nightmare?"

He nodded. "I dreamed a big hand was reaching out to grab my face." He turned on his side, his back to the light, and was immediately asleep.

We tiptoed out and shut the door. "That scream went right through me," Liz said, weak with relief. "It's not like him to have nightmares."

"I'll bet you'll find out in the morning that they were gorging themselves on cheeseburgers and banana splits and pickles right after the movie."

"Something like that," Liz said. She started for the bedroom. "You've left the downstairs light on."

I went down, fixing my eyes on the table all the way down the stairs. Before I reached the downstairs hall I could see them plainly. I stood in front of the table for a minute and looked at the cherubic expressions. *I must be going crazy!* Then I noticed something that really shook me. The face nearest me, the one I was about to touch when Richard screamed, was the one that most resembled him. I turned out the light and went slowly back upstairs and into the bedroom. Liz was lying with her eyes closed. I stood and looked at myself in the mirror. Should I tell her? If there *was* something to this business of evil, and with this thing right under our roof, hadn't she a right to know?

"Ray?"

I stirred, turning around. "Thought you were asleep," I muttered.

"Is anything wrong?" she asked.

"No—why, should there be?"

She hesitated just long enough to cause me to wonder. Had *she* noticed something that she was trying to keep from *me?* Then she sighed sleepily and turned over, wriggling deeper beneath the covers. "No, I just wondered why you were standing there looking at yourself, that's all. Come on to bed. You can admire your good looks in the morning."

I undid my tie and sat down to take off my shoes. If it happened again I *would* tell her.

3

LIZ AND THE BOYS WERE STILL ASLEEP WHEN I LEFT THE
house at nine fifteen the next morning after a breakfast of
orange juice, cornflakes, and coffee. Clouds that had hung
over London the night before had given way to one of
those rare pre-autumn days with blue skies and just
enough nip in the air to make you appreciate the warmth
of the sunshine. On such a day it is impossible to feel anything but glad to be alive. The nagging thoughts about the
table which had kept me awake until the downstairs clock
struck three had faded as I walked to the Bond Street station and caught the underground.

There was a vague sense of uneasiness still, but daylight

and movement and people brought things into proper per-
spective. Something *had* happened, but whatever it was
must have some logical explanation. I remembered the
time when I was a youngster and my dad had driven us to
someplace in upper New York State where there was a
stretch of road that seemed to run uphill but was really
downhill, and he used to delight in our refusal to believe
that it was an optical illusion. To us kids, seeing was believing. The car *had* run uphill with the engine switched
off. The same thing applied to this damn table. Some optical illusion, or some kind of autosuggestion, was playing
tricks on me. Material things simply do not change from
one shape to another. Cars do not coast uphill, they only
seem to.

I got off at the Chancery Lane station and walked to the
Public Record Office. For the next hour and a half I lost
myself in poring over logs of Elizabethan privateers and
making notes. After that I had to go outside for a cigarette
because, for obvious reasons, smoking is not allowed
among so many priceless and irreplaceable manuscripts.

I was standing on the steps in the courtyard admiring
the graceful eighteenth-century lead cisterns that now
serve as flower boxes when a man come out and paused to
light a cigarette. He was about fifty-five, distinguished
looking, unmistakably English country gentleman. His
lighter refused to work so I offered him mine and we
struck up a conversation.

"Haven't I just seen you in the Round Room?" he
asked. "Yes—chap with all those ships' logs. Interested in
maritime subjects, are you?"

I told him about my research.

"How very interesting," he said. "I'm afraid mine
would be dull stuff compared with yours. I'm an ornithol-

ogist. Write books about birds, that sort of thing." He glanced at a flight of starlings squabbling as they settled over the gatehouse. "Fascinating things, though—birds. Take those starlings. Ungainly looking brutes. Damned nuisance in the city. But out in the country they're invaluable. Keep down all sorts of pests. Nature's insecticide. Know anything about birds?"

I admitted I was pretty ignorant about the feathered variety.

"Well, there you are—to each his own. By the way, I've got something that *might* interest you, though. An old *routier*, or 'rutter' as they were known. You know, an old sea chart. Been in the family for years. Sixteenth century, I believe. Some letters with it, too. One of my ancestors was one of Elizabeth's privateers. Down the Spanish Main, that sort of thing. You're welcome to borrow it if you like."

I was delighted. It was just the type of material I was looking for, and he agreed to drop it by the house some night. "It's at my country place just now. Have to dig it out. Anyway, if you'd like to let me have your address . . ."

I gave it to him and he handed me his card in return. As he went back inside I glanced at it.

Lt. Col. Sir James Willoughby Tyrell, KG,MC,CBE

No. 4, Farlane Mews   "The Shires"
Mayfair, W.1.   King's Southerton
01-989-1212   Nr. Romsey, Hants.
    King's Southerton 384

I knew what a lieutenant colonel was and I knew that the prefix "Sir" meant he was somebody to be reckoned with. But the string of letters, impressive as they were, were a mystery to me. I put the card in my wallet, crushed out my cigarette, and went back inside.

The Public Record Office closes at one o'clock on Saturdays. Knowing that Liz and the boys wouldn't be home till four or five, I took a cab to Soho and had lunch at a little Italian restaurant. Then I walked back to Leicester Square and caught the underground to Bond Street.

I had just reached home and was putting the key in the door when I heard the phone ringing. The downstairs phone was right inside the front door, on *the* table. It stopped ringing just as I picked it up. I listened to the buzzing for a second, said "hello" just in case, then hung up. If it was important they would call again. I took my briefcase into the study, which was across the hall from the kitchen at the back of the house, overlooking the patio, and sat down at my desk to look over the notes I'd made that morning.

The study and the patio were on the sunny side of the house in the afternoon and the room was warm, even for September. After a few minutes I got up and opened the window. I had just sat down again when I heard voices. Familiar voices. At first I thought they were coming from upstairs, but as I listened I realized they came from outside. I looked back at the patio but it was empty. A profusion of roses still blossomed on the back wall and for a minute I was tempted to get a deck chair and finish sorting my notes out there, but previous experience had taught me that the idyllic picture of a writer relaxing at work in a quiet garden seldom works in reality.

So I put the idea out of my mind and was settling back to my notes when the voices came again. This time I recognized them. Sybil and Father Bunting. I couldn't see them because of the high brick wall separating her garden from our patio. Nor could I really tell what they were saying. Not at first. But then they must have walked closer to our side because their voices became more distinct.

I wasn't really listening, only half-conscious of voices in the background, until I heard my name. I raised my head and listened. But there was a lull in the conversation just then and I had no idea what they had said about me. I waited a minute. Then I heard Sybil say, "What if anyone wanted to contact you by telephone?"

"They could always reach me at 352-1202," Bunting said with a chuckle. I jotted the number down on the edge of my notebook for future reference.

"How very droll," Sybil said. I was trying to puzzle out what she meant when I heard her say, "Look, Bunting—aren't these lovely?"

I heard the priest say admiringly, "Yes, they're coming along beautifully. By the way, how is hers doing?"

My ears pricked up.

"She let it die. Didn't water it."

"Pity."

"Never mind. Everything will be all right. What about him? Do you think he suspects anything?" Sybil asked.

"Not really."

I got up and went to the window just as Bunting was saying, "Look at the time! I'd better be going."

"Yes, I think it would be just as well. I'll let you know how everything goes."

I slammed the window, hard, just to let them know.

After that there was no point in trying to work. I shoved my papers aside and went to the kitchen and filled a glass with ice cubes and was looking for the Scotch when the extension phone rang in the study. Still holding the glass I went back and answered it.

"Ray?" It was Liz.

"Hey, how's it going?" I said cheerfully, pleased to hear a friendly voice for a change.

"Ray—something's happened." She sounded far away. My heart did a flip-flop.

"Have you had an accident?" I pictured a mangled car, shattered glass sparkling, bloody smears on clothes, an ambulance shrieking.

She didn't answer.

"Liz, for God's sake, tell me! Are you and the boys all right?"

Her answer was hesitant. "Yes, we're all right, Ray, but . . ." She stopped.

I let out a sigh of relief. The ice cubes were chattering against the glass as my hand shook. I sank into the chair behind the desk. "Well, thank God for that and to hell with the car as long as you three are okay."

"Oh, the car's all right. Look, Ray, I think you should come out here. Can you get a cab? We'll be in Leonard Harding's office."

Her voice dropped; she spoke quickly, trying not to be overheard. "Ray—I've got to hang up, someone's coming." The phone went dead.

I sat there for a minute, watching the beads of sweat accumulate on the glass. Then I put the phone down and took the glass back to the kitchen. What kind of a screwy performance was this? Had she had a scrap with somebody about the boys? Why couldn't she mention it over the phone? And if she and the boys were all right, then what the hell *was* it all about? It suddenly dawned on me that I would never find out if I kept standing in the kitchen. I went back to the study and dialed the number of a cab company and gave my address. A few minutes later the cab pulled up outside. As I went out the door I stole a glance at the table. The cherubs were smiling.

At the studio gate I told the watchman that I was going to meet my wife at Harding's office.

"Building fourteen, first floor." He waved the driver through.

I paid off the taxi at the door and wasted three minutes on the lower corridor, forgetting in my excitement that the English don't start numbering from the ground up as we do and that Harding's office was on the floor above. I sprinted up the paint-flaked steps and found his office halfway along the upper hall. Harding's secretary showed me to the inner office where Liz was sitting on the edge of a couch twisting her handkerchief.

"Liz!" I sat down and put my arms around her. She looked grateful for my presence but she didn't say anything. I glanced around. "Where are the boys?"

"In the viewing theater. Leonard got somebody to run through an old war film to keep them occupied while we find out about the flower."

"What flower? What the hell's this all about anyway?"

She told me. They had rehearsed the scene once and then started to shoot. The boys and John had done it the same way before—on the tape that was mistakenly erased—so there was no real problem. It was a simple take, just a shot of Eddie and Richard "picking" a plastic rose and handing it to John Dighton, then standing around and admiring it long enough to allow time to dub in the voice-over part of the commercial.

"The take went okay," Liz was saying. "No hitches. Leonard was satisfied, so that was that. We all hung around for a few minutes, talking. Then just as I was getting the boys ready to leave, John Dighton started complaining about his hand. He really was in *pain*, Ray."

"Well, what had he *done* to it?"

"Nothing. That's the strange thing. Yet when we looked at it there were blisters coming up all over the palm."

I sat back. To tell the truth I was rather annoyed about having been dragged some thirteen miles on what I had thought was a life-and-death mission, only to find out that an actor, and one I didn't particularly care for at that, had blistered his palm.

"For God's sake, Liz! Is that all? So Dighton burned his hand—so what?"

She was shaking her head.

"I'm sorry," I said quickly. "But maybe he got hold of a rose that had too much fertilizer on it or something. These things *can* burn, you know. Especially chemical f——"

"It was a *plastic* rose."

"So maybe some ingredient in the plastic reacted on his dainty actor's hand! I still don't see any reason for the four-alarm routine."

"Ray, *please!* Just let me finish, will you?! Somebody went for a first-aid kit, but before they got back the blisters were spreading all over his hand. You could stand there and watch them *grow*. And as soon as they started to put salve on it, his . . ."—she closed her eyes and bit her lip to shut out the memory— ". . . his fingers . . . started . . . swelling."

"Where is he now, in the hospital?"

Liz nodded. "But before . . . before they got him into

the ambulance . . . Oh my God, Ray, the screams."

"Why didn't they give him a shot of something?"

"They did. Morphine. Twice. But it didn't help much. They had to strap him down."

The door opened just then and Leonard Harding came in. He nodded.

"Well?" Liz asked.

"I've just spoken to the hospital. His right arm is swollen terribly. They've decided to amputate to stop whatever it is from spreading."

"Any idea what caused this?" I asked.

Harding shook his head.

A worried-looking young man came in: the kind you see around TV and film studios—pale pink shirts, long hair, aesthetic faces.

"Yes, Frankie?" Harding said.

"We've just played back the take. I'm afraid we'll have to do it again, Mr. Harding."

"What! What the hell went wrong? It looked perfect to me. Absolutely perfect. Who dropped the can *this* time?"

Frankie shifted from one foot to the other, glanced at Liz and me, then looked back at Harding as if half-expecting not to be believed. "Nobody, Mr. Harding. But when we ran it back there was . . . no rose."

Liz and I looked at each other.

Harding took his pipe from his mouth slowly. "What the hell are you talking about, Frankie? I was watching on the monitor. I *saw* the bloody rose!"

"On the monitor, maybe. But it didn't come up on the videotape. Believe me. There's just nothing there."

"This I've got to see!" Harding said, starting for the door. Liz and I followed them out.

The tiny viewing theater was filled to overflowing by

the time we got there. Word of this bizarre business had spread through the studio. Harding made room for us and found us a couple of seats beside him. "Okay," he called in a defiant voice, "run it!"

It was the first time I had seen Eddie and Richard on the screen. They were, I was forced to admit, photogenic. But I had little time to dwell on fatherly pride. Like everyone else I was looking for the rose. We saw Eddie pick up *something* from the mock-up of a garden wall, but when he admired it for a moment before passing it to Richard . . . there was simply nothing there. John Dighton came on screen, smiling like a benevolent father. The boys were grinning up at him proudly as Richard held out his empty hand as though giving him something and John took the nothing as though something were actually there. Then all three stood admiring this thing that should have been a rose while Dighton turned it this way and that in his hand. When the clip ended and the lights went up there was a buzz of voices in the viewing room. I looked at Liz and she looked at me. I looked at Harding. He was sitting there frowning, his pipe forgotten between his teeth. Then he sat up, as if suddenly aware of the hubbub around him.

"All right, everybody out! This isn't a bloody sideshow!"

As the chastened curious shuffled obediently toward the door I asked Harding what he made of it.

"It's just bloody impossible, that's all! I *saw* the rose when we were shooting this scene. They've got the rose in the prop room. Come on, let's see what the hell this is all about."

We trailed him through various corridors, walking fast, saying nothing, each trying to fathom what could be happening. There was a crowd around the door of the prop room also, but once inside there were only Harding, Liz, myself, the property girl, and a doctor. The property girl looked frightened. When I saw what the doctor was examining with a magnifying glass I understood why.

On the table at the end of the prop room were stored racks of plastic flowers of every description, carefully sorted, each labeled according to type. But in the rack in front of the doctor was a single . . . well, it might have been a plastic rose once, but now it had melted into a cancerous-looking mass. It bore some resemblance to a plant, but it looked like no plant I had ever seen. The predominating colors, which were now mingling in a kind of congealing blob, were poisonous green, shiny black, and dark blood red.

The doctor looked up. "*I* won't touch it," he said firmly. "Not even with rubber gloves. This young lady swears it was almost like this when she came back to look for it, but it has been showing signs of gradual deterioration ever since."

"Have you heard the latest?" Harding asked the doctor. "This thing didn't even record on the videotape. Everything else went okay—but no bloody rose."

The doctor shook his head. "Damnedest thing I've ever seen."

In all this concern over Dighton there was one vital thing I had overlooked. It struck me suddenly and I grabbed Liz by the arm. "The boys! They both handled the rose!"

"No, it's all right," the doctor said. "I've got a nurse with them. She'll bring them to me immediately if anything shows up. But I've already examined them thoroughly and they seem to have escaped completely."

I was flabbergasted. "But, how . . . ? I mean, if it affected Dighton like that why wouldn't it affect them?"

The doctor shrugged. "Why didn't it affect the prop girl? There must be some epidermal sensitivity in Dighton's makeup—some subcutaneous hormone or something else we don't know about that triggered some chemical reaction in this plastic rose. Anyway, we'll impound the entire lot of these plastic flowers until we get to the bottom of this thing."

"You're sure our sons will be all right?"

"Well, I can't *guarantee* anything, Mr. Armacost. There's absolutely no medical precedent for this. But since they haven't shown any reaction I would say they're in the clear. It's been over four hours since they handled the rose." He took a card from his wallet and gave it to me. "But if anything *should* happen, ring your own doctor and then phone me. Perhaps I might have some clue by then."

Harding took us to the viewing theater where the boys had been watching their film. It had just ended and they were coming out as we got there. The nurse said they seemed to be all right, but Liz insisted they hold out their hands.

"Aw, Mom . . . !" they groaned.

The nurse laughed. "I'm afraid I've been doing that every five minutes. But I honestly believe they're in no danger."

"Of course not," Eddie said. Something in the way he said it sounded as though he *knew* nothing could happen to him.

Driving back to Bentley Square, Liz said, "Poor John Dighton."

In the rear-view mirror I saw Eddie and Richard exchange smiles.

"It isn't funny!" I said angrily.

"We weren't laughing about that, Dad," Eddie said in a tone of injured innocence.

"I'm sorry. I guess I'm on edge."

There was very little conversation the rest of the way home. I dropped them in front of the house and drove around the corner to the mews garage we had rented. Walking back I couldn't help thinking about that damn table. I felt certain it had something to do with what had happened. It might sound like silly superstition, but I was actually beginning to believe that the thing *was* evil.

As I crossed the square I saw Sybil go up to our door and ring the bell. Richard let her in. I stopped and for some reason a chill feeling came over me.

I began to think about the relationship between Sybil and Father Bunting. A priest and a middle-aged . . . A middle-aged what? Spinster? She called herself—or allowed herself to be called—Mrs. Rodne, but it had never been said in so many words so we didn't really know. Well, whatever she was—spinster, widow, or divorcée—it was strange that she should be so thick with a Catholic priest. I crossed the street toward our front door feeling a little less than charitable toward our next-door neighbor.

I was just starting up the steps when I stopped again. A snatch of their conversation was stirring in my mind, trying to surface. What *was* it? Bunting had said something about the time and that he thought he ought to be going. And Sybil had said . . . yes, by God! She had said, *"I'll let you know how everything goes."* They had known something had been going to happen because she had definitely said, "I'll let you know how everything goes."

I fumbled for my key and opened the door. The first

thing I did was look at the table. The faces were in their cherubic mood. If anything, they seemed to be smiling a little more than usual.

Voices were coming from the drawing room. I closed the front door quietly and listened. Sybil was speaking in a low voice.

"Then what happened?" she almost whispered.

I heard Edward answer, "His fingers started to swell up."

There was a pause. Then Sybil said, almost nonchalantly, "I see."

I heard a noise and turned. Liz had come out of the kitchen with a tray of tea things and was looking at me strangely. "What on earth are you doing, Ray—eavesdropping?"

"I've just come in," I said, trying to keep my voice natural.

Liz started past me. "Well come on in a little further and have a cup of tea."

I stayed in the hall. "Liz, I'd like to talk to you."

She was putting the tray on the coffee table. "Sybil is here," she said pointedly, looking at me over her shoulder.

"Yes," I said. "I know."

"Oh, my goodness," I heard Sybil laugh. "He doesn't sound very pleased."

That did it. I had to go in. Until such time as I had more to go on I couldn't afford to upset the applecart. "I'm sorry, Sybil," I said with as much sincerity as I could muster. "We've just been through a rather harrowing ordeal and I'm not myself."

Edward and Richard were sitting looking at Sybil like two schoolboys listening to a favorite teacher.

"Well, I think it's time we had something to cheer us up," Liz said. "Wait till you hear what Sybil has to say about the table."

"The table?" I looked at Sybil.

"Yes, I've got some rather exciting news. I have a friend who's very knowledgeable on antiques. He acts as consultant for some of the big galleries and places like Sotheby's. Well, anyway—I hope you don't mind, but I told him about this table of yours. It is rather unusual, isn't it—I mean, the faces and everything?"

"Faces?"

"Yes—oh, I don't know anything about antiques myself, Ray. You know that. Goodness, all you have to do is look at my house to tell that. To me a piece of furniture is something you use to sit on, sleep in, or eat from and that's that."

"The table," I said, trying to bring her back on track. "You described the faces, you say?"

"Everything. As well as I could. Anyway, Claremont said—his name is Claremont Gilpatrick—Claremont said it sounded as if it might be genuine. He asked if he might come and have a look at it, and I said I didn't think you'd mind if . . ."

"He can have the goddamn thing for all I care," I said and walked over to the cupboard where I kept the Scotch.

"No, Dad—please don't get rid of the table!" It was Eddie.

I turned to look at him. He was on the verge of tears, I swear it. So, when I looked, was Richard.

"Ray, we're having *tea*," Liz said.

"I need a drink," I said stubbornly.

"Ray, what's got into you?"

"Nothing. I'm sorry—it must be this business about

John Dighton." I excused myself, saying I had some notes to type up, and went to the study and closed the door. I sat down at my desk but any thought of work was far from my mind. I swiveled the chair around and stared for a long time at the evening shadows creeping across the patio.

I was still sitting there half an hour later, my drink untouched on the desk, an unlit cigarette in my hand, when Liz came in. Outside, it had started to rain. I hadn't even noticed. Dusk had set in, the room was almost dark.

"Ray?"

I stirred and turned around. She gave me an anxious look. "Are you all right?"

"I'm not sure," I said. "There are times lately when I think I must be going nuts."

"Is it because of what happened to John?"

"Partly." I hesitated, uncertain whether to broach what was on my mind. But it would have to come out sooner or later. Now seemed as good a time as any. "Liz, sit down. I want to talk to you."

She sat, almost timidly, choosing a straight-backed chair. She sat on the edge, very erect, hands folded in her lap, her face still wearing that worried look as she waited for me to go on. I was trying to think of a way to put it to her that wouldn't sound absurd. Some way which would let her know what had been happening without frightening her into thinking I was going screwy.

"Can we turn on a light?" She asked finally. "It's getting dark."

I switched on the desk lamp and our eyes met across the pool of light.

"Liz," I began, plunging straight in, "have you noticed anything peculiar about . . . about that table?"

She tensed just a little. "No. Why?"

"Remember the first time we saw it—those ugly gargoyles?"

"Of course I remember, darling."

I found that careful "darling" a bit disconcerting. As if she were trying to placate me.

"Have you ever . . ." I hesitated again. This was the part I didn't like, the part that would make me feel that something *was* wrong with me if she gave the wrong answer. "Have you ever seen those faces since?"

"No," she said quietly.

I waited for her to go on. The fact that she didn't made me more uneasy. Any other time she would have laughed and said, "Have *you?*" or even made a little joke about my seeing things. But this calm "no," as though she were afraid to upset some delicate balance by saying more, was unnerving.

"Well *I* have," I said. It sounded defensive.

Liz swallowed. "We—decided it was a trick of light, didn't we? Or maybe it isn't even the same table, in spite of what the boys said. Maybe the man had two and sent the other one instead."

I put my head in my hands and groaned. "Liz, don't play games. We both *know* it's the same table. *Don't we?*"

There was a moment. Our eyes met and held. She nodded. "Yes, Ray, it's the same table." But I couldn't tell if she meant it.

I jumped up. "Then you *have* seen the faces again! Don't be afraid to say it, Liz. I know how you feel—I thought I was going nuts, too. But they're *there*. Sometimes they're there, sometimes they're not. Isn't that the way?"

She looked at me sadly. "No, Ray—I've got to tell the

truth. I have not seen those horrible faces since that morning in Portobello Road. But I have seen you staring at that table when you didn't know I was looking."

If she had suddenly slapped my face I couldn't have been more astonished. I came around the desk slowly, the feeling of uneasiness growing as I realized that my reactions to this damned table had become so curious that my wife had been covertly watching me.

"Liz—believe me. There *is* something strange about that table." I laid my hand on her shoulder. It was meant to be a casual gesture, a man-and-wifely thing, to establish contact between us. Her shoulder flinched, only briefly, but it was enough to let me know how things stood. I went back and sat behind my desk, fighting down the panic. More than anything right now I wanted to be believed. Because . . . because now I wasn't really *sure*.

There was only one way. Tell her what had happened. She would *have* to believe me.

So I told her. Starting with the night of the dinner party when Mary Jane Coates had noticed the faces, too. And how after Liz had gone upstairs to bed and I stayed down to put away the liquor the faces had come back, and when I started to touch one Richard screamed out in his nightmare.

"But surely that was all coincidence, darling!" Liz said carefully, as though trying not to upset me. "The hall light throws the faces into shadow and they . . . well, seem to change."

"I thought so, too. At first. But Liz, just go back over that evening and recall what happened. The phone call came for the kids to go back and do a retake of that TV commercial. And John Dighton just *happened* to be here? It was right after Dighton had been to the phone that Mary

Jane was on her way back from the john and noticed the faces."

"But Ray, darling—I *heard* Mary Jane when she left. You had apparently *told* her it was just a trick of the light, because she said, 'Yes, I see what you mean.' And she said it was quite a pretty table."

"Of course she said that!" I snapped. "I knew the faces *had* changed because I went out for a look. But I couldn't let her know the ones she saw had actually *been* there. My God, what do you suppose would happen if word got out about this?"

Liz had that distant look again. Hesitantly she asked, "But doesn't that just prove what I said? Mary Jane *thought* they looked grotesque in the shadow, but when you went out and turned on the light they were quite normal."

There was something in what she said. I sat quietly for a moment, trying to remember just how it had happened. I *had* switched on the front hall light for a better look, and that was when the faces took on their cherubic look. But I wasn't going to give up that easily. I was firmly convinced that there was more to it than just optical illusion.

"Liz, I'm sorry, but I've got to get to the bottom of this!" That look came again and I held up my hand. "No, don't look at me as if I were crazy. Maybe I am, but it's going to take a lot to prove it to me. I haven't told you everything. I haven't told you about that priest and Sybil. Doesn't it strike you that they're a strange pair?"

Liz frowned. It was a good sign. At least it was a familiar reaction. "Oh, I don't know. She's a bit eccentric about her flowers, but I don't think there's anything—well, you know, between her and Father Bunting. They're both intellectual and like to discuss philosophy and religion. But that doesn't make them strange."

"Her flowers," I said. "You've seen some of the poisonous-looking things she grows! And as for deep philosophical discussions, I overheard them talking just this afternoon. I was sitting here with the window open when they were talking in the garden, just the other side of the wall. They were talking about your having let that hideous plant die for lack of water. And *she* said something like 'everything would be all right.'

"Do you know what I think? I think there is some connection between them and that damned table and those weird flowers and what happened to poor old Dighton."

Liz shook her head, stopping me in mid-sentence.

"Oh, Ray, you really are overreacting. I happen to know all about what Sybil and Father Bunting were talking about out there this afternoon." Liz came around the desk and sat on the arm of my chair, her hand gently massaging my neck.

"You've probably forgotten as usual, but next week is our wedding anniversary . . ."

"I hadn't forgotten!" Well, almost hadn't.

"I mentioned to Sybil that we had been married fourteen years and she, bless her, said she and Father Bunting would like to give us something."

"Give us something? But, hell—they hardly know us and she's already given us that mirror."

"Darling, our being friendly with those two has meant a lot to them. Bunting says most people steer clear of a priest, and because he's always writing and reading he rarely gets a chance to make new friends. It isn't as though he has a parish to look after—in many ways, he says, it's very lonely being an intellectual theologian. And when you treated him just like anybody else—especially that day you met at the British Museum—well, he was really quite touched. As for Sybil, do you know she told me that since she's been living in that house we're the first neighbors who've even been friendly with her?"

"That still doesn't explain the way they were talking about us this afternoon."

"There's a perfectly good explanation for what they said. Sybil has this absolutely lovely Georgian spinet in her back bedroom. She says it's in her way and a dust trap and she'd like to get rid of it—which was just her way of trying to get me to accept it as an anniversary present. But she had to tell me because she knows how proud men sometimes are about accepting things. So we planned to have a little surprise for you. We were going over to her place for drinks next week and it was going to happen then. So that was why you heard her ask Father Bunting if he thought you suspected anything, and why he said he didn't think you did. Now, don't you feel better?"

I must admit I did. In fact, I felt a little guilty about some of the things I'd said. "Maybe I let my imagination run away with me."

Liz smiled. "Come on and let's both have a drink." She kissed me and jumped up. I got up to open the door. "There's just one thing I don't understand," I said. "Shortly after we got that table Sybil said it looked 'genuine,' and she said she thought we'd got a bargain, and that it was probably worth a lot of money."

"Well?"

"Well, just an hour ago she said she *didn't* know anything about antiques and was having this guy Gilpatrick come and have a look at it."

Liz wrinkled her nose, always a dead giveaway.

"What is it, out with it—you're keeping something back," I said.

"Well, Sybil does really know quite a lot about antiques—that business a while ago was just for your benefit. It was I who asked her to get somebody to come and have a look at the table."

"Why, for God's sake?"

"Because . . . well, when I saw you were beginning to have a thing about the table I was afraid you might want to get rid of it. And that would break the boys' hearts because they're so proud of having given it to me. So I asked Sybil if she really thought it was valuable and she said she did, but if I wanted her to she would get this friend of hers to come and value it for us. That way I thought that, if it *is* valuable, you might want to keep it."

"Okay," I laughed, "you win. I'm outnumbered. And I promise I won't mention that damn table again."

The phone on my desk rang. Liz was closest to it and picked it up.

"Who? Oh, yes, doctor."

She listened for a minute, her face grave. "Oh, my God!" she whispered. I went to her but she opened her eyes and shook her head to let me know she was all right as she continued to listen. "Thank you for calling, doctor," she said finally and hung up.

"Dighton?"

She nodded, dropping heavily into my swivel chair and putting her face in her hands.

"Did they amputate?"

Again she nodded.

"How is he?" I asked.

"He's dead."

"*Dead?*"

"The amputation didn't stop the swelling. Whatever it was. It kept right on going—all over his body."

"Oh, my God!" I knelt beside her and slid an arm around her waist. "What a hell of a way to go."

"They—they couldn't stop him screaming."

She was trembling all over. I got up, trying to put the picture out of my mind. I patted her arm. "I'll bring you a drink."

She nodded. "There's more. The rose. They put it in a lead box and took it to some member of the Royal Botanical Society to identify."

She looked at me. "When they opened the box, it was gone."

"You mean—*all* gone?"

"Nothing left. Not a speck."

"I'll bring those drinks," I said and went out into the hall. As I walked toward the drawing room Eddie leaned over the banister and called down, "Hey, Dad, ask Mom when's supper. We're starved."

"It won't be long. We're just going to have a quick drink first. There's been some bad news. John Dighton just died in the hospital."

"Yeah, we know," Richard piped from behind Eddie.

I stopped and looked up. "How did you know?"

"Aw—we heard you talkin'. You can hear everything in this old house! Come on, Eddie, show me how to make a rabbit snare the way you promised!" The door slammed. I went into the living room and mixed two drinks. Very stiff ones. Especially mine.

SUNDAY WAS A LOST DAY. LIZ WAS STILL IN A STATE OF mild shock over what happened to John Dighton. I wasn't much better. We slept late, then took the boys to the London Zoo in the afternoon. It was bright and sunny, but even this couldn't dispel the depression that hung over us like a cloud. We came home early, had supper, watched TV for a while, and went to bed at nine thirty. The weather changed suddenly overnight. Southwest gales battered the southern coast of England. At breakfast the radio news listed a mounting toll of damage to coastal resort towns. A Danish trawler was driven aground at Portland Bill and all hands lost. Fallen trees blocked highways and railroad lines. The Exeter Express was derailed near Temple Combe.

Even our usually sheltered square felt the force of the winds. Trees whiplashed about, bobbing and weaving in the driving rain. Inside the house drafts sprang from nowhere, rattling doors and windows and making little moaning noises under the eves. From the breakfast table we could see the desolation inside the walled patio: garden furniture overturned, climbing roses torn from the walls, and a miniature river of muddy water coursing over the flagstones. I could understand how primitive man had linked nature's wrath and the displeasure of the gods. In my secret heart I felt there could *be* some strange connection between this furious onslaught and the fate of John Dighton. But I did not say it out loud.

When Liz and the boys had left the house, buttoned up in plastic raincoats and Wellington boots, I took a pot of coffee into the study and settled down to work. But I found my mind wandering. I read absentmindedly through part of my notes and after about an hour I found I'd doodled my way through a pot of coffee and done absolutely nothing toward organizing my material. I got up and made a fresh pot of coffee.

I had just returned to the study when the phone rang.

"Is that Mr. Armacost?"

"Yes."

"James Tyrell here."

James Tyrell? Who the hell was James Tyrell?

"I had to come down to the country last night and I remembered I'd promised to dig up that *routier* we were talking about the other day."

I remembered then. "Oh—yes, Sir James."

"Well, I've found it—and also a packet of letters from

some privateering ancestor of mine. I'm driving back to town this morning, providing the roads are clear—deuced storm down here last night: trees down, that sort of thing—and if you think these might be of any use to you I can drop them off at your place."

"That's very kind of you, Sir James. Look, why don't you stay and have dinner with us?"

"Most generous of you, old chap, but I'm giving one of my infamous bird lectures—on chaffinches—to a group of enthusiasts in Stepney tonight. But I'd be delighted to make it some other time. Would it be inconvenient if I dropped these things by your place about half-past two?"

"Not at all. I'm in all day."

"Right. Look forward to seeing you. Cheerio."

One slides into the idiom. I found myself replying "cheerio" before I realized it. I hung up smiling when I thought how that would go down back home.

He was as good as his word. The doorbell rang as the carriage clock in the drawing room struck half-past two. I opened the door and he blew in on a rainy gust, dripping wet and carrying a plastic-wrapped package.

"What a frightful day!" he exclaimed as I helped him out of his dripping raincoat. "I suppose it's living up to what you expect English weather to be like, eh?"

I laughed. "I understand it's 'unusual.' "

"Bound to be. We never have anything but 'unusual' weather. England has the best climate and the worst weather in the world. I say, what an extraordinary table! Those faces—positively make your flesh creep. Italian, isn't it? Foreign, anyway."

I looked at the table. Cherubs. I swear it.

I told him to go into the drawing room while I hung up his raincoat. Then I stole another look at the table.

Cherubs. Definitely. So it *was* an optical illusion. I went to join Sir James.

We had a drink, talked for a while, and then he opened the package. It contained an old sea chart dated 1578 on which was marked the cruise of a ship called the *Southwind* along the Spanish Main in 1580–82. There was also the *Southwind*'s log, leatherbound, the entries in a precise but florid hand, the ink now sepia with age. On the flyleaf was written: "*Southwind—Captain Sir James Tyrell.*"

"He was a proper scoundrel," Sir James said of his namesake with more pride than denigration. "Family cupboard's full of skeletons. This chap was a privateer, as you probably gathered. Letters patent from Good Queen Bess herself. The ship was originally a Spaniard. The *Miraflores*, I think. The old boy took her as a prize in some engagement or other and borrowed to the hilt to fit her out himself. He came to a sticky end, though. Crew mutinied off the West Indies and abandoned ship. Left old Sir James lashed to the wheel stark naked and cut to ribbons. British man-of-war found him. Quite dead of course. It's all there somewhere—his letters, some from his widow. If it's of any use to you keep the stuff as long as you like."

I was delighted. Here was authentic material, enough background for at least one novel in my series, and I could refer to it at will without having to make laborious piecemeal notes in some archives or other. I tried to express my thanks.

"Nonsense, old chap. Glad the stuff is of some use to you. The only thing of interest I came across was an entry in the log—you'll probably see it when you go through it—about one of the crew reporting a great tit resting in the rigging somewhere off the coast of South America. Most unusual. Wouldn't have believed it—they're nonmigratory, you know—except for the fact that old Sir James had sketched it. Climbed the rigging with pen, ink horn, and parchment to do it, mind you. Ah, they were sailors in those days. It *was* a great tit, no doubt about that. Have the drawing at home someplace. Most unusual." He glanced at his watch. "Dear me, *tempus fugit*. Must be off."

He stood up to go. I thanked him again as we went out into the hall and made a tentative engagement for dinner sometime soon. As I helped him into his coat he commented once more on the table. "Yes, must be Italian. Can't say I'd like to live with those faces though. Positively evil. Yes, that's the word. Evil. Belongs to the people you let the house from, I suppose?"

I tried to say "yes" convincingly, but I'm not a very good liar. He began to stutter with embarrassment.

"Oh, I say—do forgive me. I didn't mean to . . . I mean, it is quite a decent table. It's just that I . . ."

I burst out laughing. "Forget it, Sir James! Those faces cause quite a lot of comment. I'm used to it. Frankly, I hate the damn thing myself. The boys bought it for their mother—so we couldn't very well throw it out without hurting their feelings."

"Of course not, dear chap, of course not."

He left, darting out into the wind and rain with upturned collar and a shouted "Cheerio." I watched till he drove off, then closed the door and turned to look at the table. Cherubs. I picked up the precious manuscripts and walked back to my study, whistling.

Liz came home with the news that Sybil had arranged for her friend Gilpatrick to look at the table the following morning. "You'll be home, won't you?" she asked.

"Wouldn't miss it for the world." Actually I had planned to spend the morning at the Public Record Office where I had reserved some documents, but I could phone and cancel them. Anyway I was now completely absorbed in the *Southwind* papers and wanted to finish them.

I was in my study the following morning still reading the *Southwind* papers when the doorbell rang. I heard a man's voice and a minute later Liz stuck her head around the door. "He's here."

I left the papers and followed her into the hall.

Anyone named Claremont Gilpatrick who was an authority on antiques just had to be lean, aesthetic, goateed, and about sixty-five. He was actually about six foot two, around two-hundred and fifty pounds of solid muscle, and looked as if he might have had a good future in the prize ring. He was about thirty-five.

He was on his knees examining the table with complete absorption when I came up behind him. He didn't look up or acknowledge my presence when Liz said, "This is my husband." The feeling was that of having interrupted a priest in the act of consecration. We stood quietly for a full three minutes while he went over the table from all angles, sometimes using a magnifying glass and a pen flashlight to peer into dark corners. I felt a tickle in my throat and wondered if it would be sacrilegious to cough. Just as the tickle was becoming uncontrollable he sighed and lumbered to his feet.

"No doubt about it," he said with all the gravity of Einstein confirming $E = MC^2$. "It's absolutely genuine."

I wanted to ask "genuine what?" but didn't have the courage. Liz, brave girl, did it for me.

"Genuine what?" she asked innocently.

It must have been the feminine touch. He wreathed his

big red face in smiles and words poured out. "Early Renaissance . . . mid-fifteenth century . . . Florentine . . .
very rare in this country . . . exquisite workmanship
. . ." and so on.

"Is it worth much?" I asked. Maybe it was just that I
asked stupid questions. He gave me a look and said, "One
hesitates to place a *price* on such a work of art, sir. Price
can only be estimated. But its *value*, both as a work of art
and because of its rarity, perhaps even its *uniqueness*, is
quite another matter. From that standpoint it has consid-
erable value. Were you thinking of selling it?"

"Oh, no!" Liz jumped in quickly.

"How much do you think it would sell for?" I asked.
"At auction."

He paused. "I should say—and mind you this is only a
guess—somewhere in the region of a thousand."

"Pounds?" I gasped.

This time he looked straight down his nose at me.
"Guineas," he said coldly.

I tried to figure. "Well, a guinea is a pound and five
pence. So . . ."

"Two thousand three hundred and sixty-two dollars,"
Gilpatrick said. He was one of those people who is always
absolutely right. And lets you know it.

"I must be going," he said. "I have other appraisals to
make. That will be five guineas."

I didn't get it right away. I thought he must be evaluat-
ing the vase on the table. He was looking at it when he
said it.

"It's *half* my usual fee—as a special favor to Mrs.
Rodne."

Liz tumbled. "Just let me get my bag." She gave me a
dirty look and went into the drawing room.

"What do you think of the faces?" I asked.

"Hmm-m?" he replied, looking annoyed, down his nose.

"The faces. On the table."

He looked. "Quite right for the period."

"Gargoyles?"

He looked at me as though I'd slipped my pin. "They are called *cherubs*," he said, pronouncing it carefully, talking to the cretin again. "Gargoyles are architectural features, usually found on churches in the form of watersprouts."

"I mean—sometimes they *look* like gargoyles. Don't you think?"

He flicked out his pencil flashlight and shined it on one of the cherubs from various angles. Then the other. He flicked the light away and clasped his hands behind his back, ignoring me, staring at the ceiling. Couldn't care less. No time to humor idiots. Liz came out waving the check. "Here you are! And thank you so much for coming." He slipped the check away with a practiced movement which suggested that taking money—especially as little as five guineas—was beneath his dignity. "Thank you, madam." He went to the door before either of us could make the hostlike gesture, nodded curtly, and was gone.

"Stuffed shirt!"

"Ray—two thousand dollars!"

"A lot of money for an old table," I said, looking at it.

I went back to my study and picked up the *Southwind* papers. But I couldn't concentrate. For some reason Claremont Gilpatrick had left a bad taste in my mouth. Idly I took out the E-to-K section of the London directory and looked him up. "Gilpatrick, C., apprsr. & valur., 22

Shooters Hill Rd., SE3 . . . 858-1235." So he was for real. And he lived in a well-heeled part of town. I closed the directory. But I couldn't pick up the thread of work. He *still* stuck in my craw. On sudden impulse I looked up the number of Sotheby's auction rooms and dialed it.

When they answered I gave my name and address and went on, "I've got an antique Italian table I would like to have an opinion on. Someone gave me the name of an expert valuer to contact, but I'm afraid I wrote it on the back of a cigarette package and I've thrown it away. It was something like Kilbride or Kilpatrick."

"Oh, yes, sir. I believe you could mean Mr. Claremont Gilpatrick?"

"Yes, that's it. Er—does he work for you, or is he on his own?"

"He isn't connected with our organization, but we do ask him to do valuations for us quite often. He is perfectly reliable, sir."

"I see. Then it would be all right for me to contact him at his home, would it?"

"Well, yes it would, normally—but I'm afraid he's out of the country just now. As a matter of fact he's in Heidelberg looking over some seventeenth-century glass for us. Which makes me think, that he might not be *just* the man for your table, sir. His specialty is china and glass."

I was sitting bolt upright now. Heidelberg? Glass? "You mean he wouldn't know anything about an antique Italian table?"

"I wouldn't say he wouldn't know anything about it, but—and I'm sure Mr. Gilpatrick wouldn't mind my saying this—while he does have quite a knowledge of the whole field of antiques his specialty *is* glass and china and if you were asking for professional valuation I'm sure he would be the first to suggest that you call in one of our other appraisers who is more knowledgeable in that particular field."

"I see," I said, my mind playing leapfrog with Gilpatrick, Sybil, Bunting, and the table.

"Would you like us to do that, sir?"

I came back from my mental peregrinations. "Do what?"

"Send someone to look at your table."

That caught me off guard. I hestitated for a second. Why not? "How soon could he come?"

"Would tomorrow morning suit you? About half-past ten?"

"Could you hang on a minute? I just want to check with my wife."

I sauntered into the kitchen. It was almost lunchtime. Liz was chopping onion for the avocado salad. "It's not ready yet, darling," she said. "Getting hungry?"

"No, I just came to ask if you're doing anything special tomorrow morning."

"I've got an appointment to have my hair done at ten. But I can put it off if you need me for something."

"No. Just curious, that's all. Give me a shout when soup's ready." I went out casually, picking up a lettuce leaf to chew on. Back in the study I snatched up the phone. "Yes, that will be fine. Ten thirty tomorrow morning."

I hung up and sat back, feeling just a little bit guilty. It was one thing to be suspicious of a garrulous and interfering neighbor like Sybil Rodne, but there is something degrading about suspecting your own wife. I tried to shake off the feeling by telling myself that of course Liz knew nothing about it. She had probably told Sybil that I hated the table and would like to get rid of it. And that would worry Liz because it might upset the boys. So Sybil, always a little too anxious to help out, probably suggested the valuation. Only to play it safe, just in case the table *wasn't* worth very much, Sybil, without telling Liz, had probably briefed a friend to act as a valuer, even to the point of picking the name Claremont Gilpatrick out of the phone book in case I checked, and told him to put a price on it that would make me want to hang onto it. The question now was—did I tell Liz, or did I keep quiet?

I elected to keep quiet. At least for the moment. I don't know why. Perhaps because I had already let Liz see how suspicious I was of Sybil and to do it again might appear paranoid.

We were having lunch a few minutes later when a thought suddenly struck me. Sybil had asked Bunting, *"Do you think he suspects anything?"* and Bunting had replied, *"Not really."*

"How do you like the avocado salad?" Liz asked.

I stirred out of my reverie. "Haven't tasted it yet." I sampled a mouthful. "Good!" Then my taste buds began to prickle.

"What's wrong?" Liz asked.

"It's got a funny taste."

"It's a new dressing. Sybil gave me the recipe and some herbs from her garden to make it with."

I was sorry I had swallowed it. I could feel a strange reaction rippling my esophagus. Purely psychosomatic. Maybe.

"Do you like it?" I asked.

"You know I don't like herbs. I stick to chopped onion and Worcester on my avocado."

"Then why the hell experiment on me?" I shouted and

threw down my spoon. "How do you know she isn't trying to poison us all?"

Liz looked at me, saying nothing for a moment. "I made
it because you *like* herbs. You *always* ask me to put extra
sage in your sausage, and bay leaf in your stew, and I told
Sybil you liked herbs. She was only trying to be neighborly! Why do you have to keep *picking* on her?"

The phone rang. Liz got up to answer it, flinging down
her napkin.

"I'll get it, Liz," I said. But she was already out of the
room, her annoyance lying heavy in her wake. I listened
till I heard her pick up the phone, then I tiptoed to the
sink, scraped the dressing out of the hollow center of the
avocado, and flushed it quietly down the drain. I went
back to the table and had wolfed down nearly half the avocado by the time she returned.

"It's for you," she said distantly and sat down, picking
primly at her food.

"Who is it?"

"Mr. Ormsby Henniker-Harnsworth."

"The headmaster? What on earth does he want?"

"I didn't ask," Liz said. "He said he wanted to speak to
you, so I assume he is aware that you wear the pants in
this family and that anything concerning *your* sons will be
discussed between the two of you in typical male-
chauvinist fashion and only passed on to the boys' mother
if it is deemed suitable for her ears."

"Oh, Liz—for God's sake!" This time I threw down my
napkin and got up.

In the hall I snatched up the phone and barked, "Yes?"

"Mr. Armacost, would it be convenient for you to drop
by my study as soon as possible? There is something I
would like to discuss with you."

His tone was one he might use with one of his pupils and he had chosen the wrong time to use it with me. "No, it is *not* convenient," I said sharply. "I'm a busy man. Can't we discuss it now?"

His voice took on an edge and I got the feeling that he was angry and controlling it. I was sorry I had let my own annoyance show. It gave him an advantage. "I'd rather not discuss it over the telephone, and I think you will agree when you hear what it is, Mr. Armacost. I prefer to keep matters of this sort within the school if possible. It always causes an unsavory atmosphere if one brings in the police."

"Police?"

"Yes, Mr. Armacost. The police. Shall I expect you?"

"Yes, I'll be there."

I hung up and went back to the kitchen. There is nothing to heal a family breach like an attack from the outside. One minute Liz was sitting there, coolly ignoring me. Then I told her, "The boys must have done something. He was talking about calling the police if I didn't come." She was on her feet, her eyes searching mine, all petty animosity forgotten. "Ray, whatever's happened?"

"I haven't a clue." I went to get my raincoat in the hall, calling back over my shoulder, "Would you like to come with me?"

"Did he ask me?"

"No, but what the hell—you're their mother."

"I'll come, but I'd better wait in the car. It might be something he wouldn't want to talk about in front of me."

The rain was pelting down, whipped by a gusty wind as we drove through the school gates and up the graveled drive. I left Liz in the car and pushed my way into the wind onto the portico and rang the bell. The same sad-faced flunky ushered me in, this time giving me a sideways glance of curiosity as he hung my coat on the hall tree. Henniker-Harnsworth still crouched behind his expanse of Edwardian desk, but there was not even a limp, damp handshake on this occasion. He dismissed the flunky with a nod, pointed curtly to a chair for me to be seated, and got straight to the point.

"I'll not mince words, Mr. Armacost. If it were not for your sons' scholastic ability, and for the fact that they came to St. Bartholomew's well recommended . . ."

And by a well-heeled source, I thought, you old bugger.

". . . I would insist on their instant dismissal. But I . . ."

"Would you mind telling me just what they've done, first," I said.

"They played a very stupid prank, which except for a fortunate oversight, could have cost a man his life."

I felt sick. Sick and angry.

"What happened?"

Henniker-Harnsworth clamped his hands over his paunch and tilted back his swivel chair. "We have an elderly caretaker named Forest. He stokes the boilers, does the lawns, that sort of thing. Quite often, as happens in all schools with a normal quota of lively boys, Forest is the butt of the occasional schoolboy prank. Usually he takes these things in stride, despite the fact that he has a weak heart. Sometimes he even manages to get his own back on the lads with no hurt feelings on either side. Tit for tat. I think he quite enjoys it, actually. But this morning when he came to work he went into the boiler house to stoke the fires and when he tried to pick up the huge poker that he uses he found it was held in place by a piece of copper wire. At first he thought someone had simply played a joke by trying to wire it to the wall. Then he saw that the wire came from one of the electrical circuits. The floor was wet from water that had flooded under the door during last night's downpour. He would have been immediately electrocuted—except that the pranksters had switched off the current at the main fuse box in order to do the wiring and had apparently forgotten to switch it on again afterward."

My mouth felt dry. "And what makes you think my boys did this thing?"

"The games master remembered seeing them sneaking out of the boiler house after classes yesterday."

"But that doesn't prove that they . . ."

He leaned forward with his arms on his desk, his smile positively triumphant. "My dear Mr. Armacost—they have already admitted it."

What do you say at a time like that? Your kids have pulled a stupid joke that nearly cost a man his life. You know they didn't mean anything serious to happen, but that doesn't detract from the seriousness of the act. You feel that you could kick their butts, but at the same time you feel they should be spared the almost gleeful Dickensian revenge of a man like Henniker-Harnsworth.

I sighed. "What do we do now?"

"Naturally I want you to have a word with your lads, just to satisfy yourself of their guilt. Then I would like your permission to let the school deal with this in the usual way."

"The usual way?"

"Six strokes each across the backside with a thin malacca cane. Painful, but not disabling."

I thought about that for a minute. "Do you normally get

the parents' permission before applying corporal punishment?"

He spread his hands. "No—but under the circumstances . . ."

I was beginning to see it now. "What circumstances?" I asked testily.

He became embarrassed then. "Why, er—you do come from abroad, Mr. Armacost, and . . . well, naturally we like to keep up good relations with . . ."

"Look, Mr. Henniker-Harnsworth, don't try to kid me. You have boys here who are the sons of titled Englishmen and foreign ambassadors and oil sheiks. I'm sure you don't bother to contact *their* fathers each time you feel corporal punishment is necessary."

"That's beside the point."

"That's precisely the point."

He got red in the face then. "There is no need to be quite so belligerent, Mr. Armacost."

"There is every reason. If my sons have broken the school rules, and those rules call for specific punishment, then they have got guts enough to take what's coming to them and I am man enough to accept that. But on the other hand I am not going to let my boys think that I was brought here to lend weight to your application of punishment. If they deserve punishment, then that is a matter to be handled by you and your school. I will deal with them in my own way when they come home."

I stood up to go, feeling really angry now.

"Don't you want to question the boys?"

"I'll talk to them at home."

I didn't wait for formal good-byes. I went out into the hall and let his door slam behind me. As I turned the corner I barged straight into a youngish man with a dark mustache who was wearing a master's gown. The impact nearly knocked him off his feet. I muttered an apology and went out the front door, turning up my collar as I ran through the driving rain toward the car.

Liz was stunned when I told her. "The little idiots! They could have killed the man."

"It was just a kid thing. But it was a damn stupid thing to do. They deserve a good hiding, and if old Henniker-Harnsworth hadn't pussyfooted around because of Haliburton's money I'd have told him to lay on an extra one for me."

Liz was silent for a moment, watching the traffic as we stopped for the lights. "Ray, when they come home don't be too hard on them. They will have had their punishment."

"I know Liz. But it is a serious matter and I can't just let it pass without saying anything."

"No, I suppose not," she sighed.

I was in the study with the *Southwind* papers when the boys came home from school later that afternoon. I could hear the murmur of their voices as they talked to Liz in the hall. A couple of minutes later there was a knock and Liz stuck her head into the study. "Eddie and Richard have got something to tell you."

They came in, a bit sheepishly, standing first on one foot and then the other. "Well?" I said.

"We got a licking at school today," Eddie said.

"Both of you?"

They nodded in unison.

"What for?"

"Oh, we played a trick on old Forest."

"What kind of trick and who's Forest?"

"He's a kind of janitor. We hooked up a couple of electric wires to give him a shock—you know, just a little jolt, for fun—but I guess we forgot they've got 230 volts over here and . . . well, with the floor being wet and everything it could've killed him."

"Yes." Richard nodded solemnly. "It was stupid and we're really sorry, Dad."

"It was *damn* stupid," I said.

They nodded again.

"We had a good hiding for it," Eddie said.

"Oh?"

"Old Henniker-Harnsworth really laid it on with that cane."

Richard nodded in corroboration, rubbing his bottom. "Boy, he sure did. But, you know somethin', Dad? I think he kind of *enjoyed* it."

He is just the kind of bastard who would, too, I thought. Out loud I said, "Well, I'm very disappointed in you boys. But I know you well enough to know that you don't make the same mistake twice. So I'm not going to do anything. You've had your punishment. Just let it be a lesson to you."

They nodded, still solemn, and went out, closing the door behind them. I thought about it for a minute, smiled with relief, and went back to work. Some ten minutes later I got up to find Liz. As I opened the study door I could hear their voices from upstairs, muffled but clear enough to be understood. Richard was saying, "Dad's right when he says we won't make the same mistake twice."

Eddie giggled and came back with, "Yeah, next time we won't forget to turn the switch back on, huh?"

They both laughed and I heard a roughhouse start as

they wrestled off the bed onto the floor. What a weird sense of humor kids have. Thank God they couldn't mean what they said. I shook my head, and went to look for Liz.

5

THE FOLLOWING MORNING WE AWOKE TO A BLUE SKY SWEPT
clear of clouds and a day brilliant with autumn sunshine.
With the usual last-minute rush Liz got the boys out the
front door to take them to school on the way to her hair-
dressing appointment. I went back to my study and immersed myself in the *Southwind* papers which now promised to give me the basis for perhaps two or more novels in
the series. I lost all track of time and was a little surprised
when the doorbell rang and I looked at my watch to see
that it was ten o'clock. The valuer from Sotheby's had arrived half an hour early.

But when I opened the front door I found Sybil on the step.

"I've just come to congratulate you!" she said, flowing in and leaving a musky smell of perfume.

"Congratulate?"

"Yes, the table. Claremont phoned last night. I would have come over but it was such a dreadfully stormy night." She stepped back to admire the table. "Just imagine—one *thousand* guineas. Aren't you thrilled, Ray?"

"Yes, of course I am." But I was thinking that I had to get rid of her without pushing, and soon, or the man from Sotheby's would arrive and spoil everything.

"You don't *sound* very thrilled," she said.

"Oh, don't pay any attention to me. I'm always like this when I'm starting a book." I glanced at my watch. "I'd like to ask you to have some coffee, Sybil, but I've got a research assistant coming."

She took the hint. She gave a last caressing touch to the table and as she went to the door she took my hand briefly. "Ray, I'm not a gushy person, but I can't tell you what it means to me to have neighbors like you and Liz and the boys. It has brightened an old woman's life."

"Not so heavy on the 'old.' " I grinned. "You're a long way from the scrap heap yet."

"Flatterer!" she laughed.

I closed the door with a sigh of relief and went back to the study. Maybe I had her all wrong. She was just a screwy middle-aged woman who had grown kind of lonely. Okay, so she had some funny habits and grew odd plants. So what? Maybe some people thought I was strange, too, digging in archives and old manuscripts for weeks on end and then making up stories about them. Everybody is a little bit crazy.

The next time the doorbell rang it was ten thirty and I opened it to a little man with glasses and a briefcase who spoke very quietly and said his name was Monroe and that he was from Sotheby's. I showed him the table and he looked at it without comment, took out a tape measure, and began jotting down dimensions in a notebook. I asked him if he would like a cup of coffee and he murmured "yes, please" and went on with his business. When I came back with the coffee he was making a sketch of the table. He drank his coffee as he sketched; then he put away his sketch pad and started searching through his briefcase.

"Dash it, I've forgotten my torch," he said.

I took my flashlight from the alcove beside the front door and gave it to him. He thanked me and went down on all fours and began to go over the underneath side even more thoroughly than Gilpatrick had, still making notes.

"What do you think of it?" I asked finally, trying to drag some comment out of him.

"I would like to reserve judgment until I've had time to consider all aspects, if you don't mind, sir." It was not a rebuff, just a statement of fact. He was thorough, I'll say that.

When he crawled out from under the table a few minutes later and dusted himself off I tried a new tack. "Those faces," I said, "they seem to change sometimes. I think it's the light that does it."

"It's quite possible," he said, still jotting. "Some Florentine craftsmen were noted for that sort of thing. There is a story that one noble Florentine lady couldn't get her husband out of bed in the morning. So she called in a man who carved a panel for the door that was opposite the foot of the bed—carved it in such a way that when the morning sun slanted into the room the shadows made the faces of the panel look quite revolting. This so unnerved the husband that he took to getting up instead of lying in bed. But by the time evening came and the candles were lighted the faces took on a most benign look so that the lady and her husband could retire to bed with a feeling of well-being."

"I'm glad to hear that," I said more sincerely than he knew. "I was beginning to think I was going nuts."

He fell silent again, as though the telling of the story had exhausted his quota of words for the day. A few minutes later he packed his things away, picked up his hat and briefcase, and started for the door.

"Shall I write you a check?" I asked, thinking he had forgotten.

"No, no—the office will send along a statement together with my report. Good day, sir."

I closed the door and went back to the study. Regardless of what else his investigation might show, it was well worth the fee to have the reassurance that it *was* just a trick of light that made the faces change and not some unknown sinister force.

"She wants us to come for dinner. All four of us," Liz was saying.

We were having lunch in the morning room and I was compiling a list of books I wanted to look up at the Reading Room in the British Museum. "Who does?" I asked absently.

"Oh, Ray—you haven't even been listening! Sybil. Tomorrow night. For our wedding anniversary."

Our anniversary! I had almost forgotten. Under Bishop Creighton's *Queen Elizabeth* I wrote, "anniv. flowers."

"Just don't phone up from the British Museum at the last minute and say you've forgotten the dinner."

"Are the boys invited too?"

"Ray—I've just *told* you. And don't forget to be pleasantly surprised about the spinet."

She started to clear the table. "I'd like to run out to Elstree and see what's going on at the studio. Besides, I'd like to ask Leonard if there are any more clues about what happened to poor John Dighton," she added with a touch of nervousness.

"They seem to have hushed that up."

"Can you blame them? If a rumor got around that it was some kind of a disease, every production at Elstree would grind to a halt."

I walked over to Bond Street station and caught the underground to Russell Square. The Reading Room at the British Museum was filled and I had to wait for someone to leave before I could get a desk and apply for the books I wanted. When I had filled in the application tickets I wandered around examining some of the thousands of reference books lining the circular walls. The very massiveness of the Reading Room was so impressive that each time I entered there I felt depressed at the thought of the paucity of knowledge one person can accumulate in a lifetime. The soaring rotunda with its skylighted dome perched high above the hundreds of desks radiating spokewise from the center, and the feeling of hush and concentration left me with the sensation of standing in a silent human forest where learning was being sucked up by osmosis as trees absorb the rain.

To pass the time till my books arrived I decided to go to the coffee room, but before I reached the steps I collided with a man who was just coming out of the Archaic Room. We exchanged apologies and I was turning away when he said, "Aren't you Mr. Armacost?"

I turned to look at him.

"I'm Peter Headley, history master at St. Bartholomew's," he laughed. "We always seem to be bumping into each other."

I remembered then. "I'm sorry about yesterday," I told him. "I was a little upset. The headmaster and I had just had a disagreement."

He smiled. "Yes, so I heard. Look, I'd like to talk to you. Would you join me in a cup of coffee?"

We chatted about trivialities until we had settled at a table with our coffee. Then Headley got to the point. "Mr. Armacost, I would appreciate it if you wouldn't mention this meeting to the headmaster."

"Playing hookey?"

"No, nothing so dramatic. I have no classes this afternoon so I came down to arrange a tour for my history pupils for next term. My presence here is strictly legitimate. No—what I wanted to talk to you about was something quite different."

I felt a twinge of apprehension. "Has it anything to do with the prank my boys played on the caretaker?"

"Only indirectly. It was a silly thing to do, of course, but I'm afraid the Head made quite a thing of it. I'll bet he didn't tell you anything about your sons on the credit side, did he?"

"No, as I recall he was within an ace of having them expelled. If he felt there was a credit side he sure didn't mention it."

"I thought not," Headley snorted. "But you can bet he wouldn't expel them."

"Because of the Haliburton trust?" I asked. From the expression on Headley's face I could see he didn't know what I was talking about. "Forget I said that. It's school business, not mine. I shouldn't have mentioned it, only I thought you were going to say it first."

"No, I don't know anything about the school finances. And I'd rather not—just so long as they can find my pay-check each month." He grinned. "Actually, I was talking about the results of their intelligence tests. We usually give them at about ten years old. Since neither of your sons had any record of such a test we gave it to them both at once."

"You mean an I.Q. test?"

"Yes. We use an up-to-date form of the Binet test. I think it's pretty well standard. The thing is, the results came in yesterday. Just before all this fracas about the caretaker. I gave the test, so naturally I was excited about the results and wanted Henniker-Harnsworth to tell the boys and send you a letter about it."

Now I did feel apprehensive. "Don't tell me they flunked it?"

"Quite the reverse. They each came out with an I.Q. of 170—near genius."

I was staggered. Absolutely staggered. "There must be some mistake."

But Headley was taking it all very seriously. "You must understand, Mr. Armacost, that this test is a measure of their *potential*. It doesn't necessarily mean that they are au-tomatically child prodigies. When they have absorbed a little more education they may begin to show some sur-prising results. But for the moment we mustn't expect any startling philosophical or scientific pronouncements from them."

"I—I don't know what to say!" I said. And I didn't. "For one thing, how can you reconcile an I.Q. of 170 with a stupid trick like electrocuting the caretaker? That was sheer idiocy, not near genius."

He smiled. "That was boyish immaturity. As I said,

when they develop a little further, then will be the time."
He finished his coffee and glanced at his watch. "I'm glad
I met you, Mr. Armacost. It isn't often a teacher has the
privilege of finding he has near genius in his hands. It's
quite a thrill. I'm sure it must be for you, too—as their father."

"Frankly I find it a trifle disquieting." I laughed.

We both stood up to leave and as we walked back up the
steps Headley said, "By the way, I'm astonished at the
knowledge your lads have of English history. They put
some of our own boys to shame. I didn't know there was
much emphasis on the subject in American schools, especially at such an early age."

"I don't think there is," I said. "The boys have simply
taken an interest since we've been here. We've visited a
few places, old castles, stately homes, and I think the boys
found that history is not just something in a book but a reality. But I wouldn't test their knowledge too far. Most of
it has been obtained from brochures and road maps."

He laughed. "Well, it doesn't really matter how they
learned it, except that I would say theirs is the ideal
way—to be really interested in a subject. They come up
with some amazing facts nevertheless. Last week, for instance, we were doing the House of York in a small written quiz. One of the questions was the date of the murder
of the young princes in the Tower."

"Well, I know I couldn't get it right within a hundred
years," I told him.

"Few adults could, I suppose. But this is the strange
thing about your boys—because they are different ages I
take each one for history separately with his own form and
age group. So naturally they aren't both studying the same
period of history. Richard, being the younger, is on an-

cient Britain while Edward's form is doing the fifteenth century. On the question about the date of the murder of the princes, everybody—at least, those who got it right—put down August 1483. But Edward put down August 23, 1483."

"Was he right?"

"That's just the point. August is generally regarded as the *probable* month for the murder, but no one is certain. So naturally I was intrigued as to how Edward had arrived at the exact date of August twenty-third. When I asked him he merely shrugged and said he thought it was right."

"He probably made it up on the spur of the moment."

"Yes, I thought about that, too. But the curious thing is that during the following period I took Richard's form for history and I called him aside and asked if he knew the date. He gave me the same answer. Straight out, with no hesitation."

"They probably read it on the back of a package of cornflakes or something. They're always quoting from cereal boxes. In America it was moon shots or baseball statistics. I don't think *that* is any evidence of genius."

We both laughed and shook hands. "So don't worry about their being expelled. Old Henniker-Harnsworth isn't likely to get rid of genius that might one day bring honors to his beloved school."

It was just after six when I got home that evening. The October days were drawing in and it was already dark. As I went up the steps I could see the whitish-blue light of the TV through the curtains. I unlocked the door and went in, peering into the front room. The TV newscaster was interviewing a bank robber just out of prison who was complaining that dole money was hard to live on. The room was empty. There was a light in the kitchen and a delightful smell of steak and onions. I went to find Liz.

She was standing with her back to me watching the steaks under the grill, her new hairdo protected by a bandeau, a frilly apron around her waist. I stood in the doorway for a minute admiring her legs before she noticed me and gave a little gasp. "God, you scared the life out of me!"

I went over and gave her a kiss. "Next time I'll ring the bell."

"Dinner's almost ready. See if the boys have set the table, will you?"

On my way to the study I stuck my head around the dining-room door. "Perfect!" I called out to her. They had even remembered the napkins and the ice water. I put my stuff away in the study, washed my hands, and went back to the kitchen.

"How did it go at the studio?"

She frowned. "Things are pretty slack. The film business is in a bad way financially. They're having trouble finding backing for productions."

I stole an olive from the salad mix. "I'm not surprised. They've poured too much money into a lot of garbage that just didn't recoup at the box office. Where're the boys?"

"Watching the boob tube. Can't you hear it?"

"No they're not. I just looked."

She began sliding steaks onto a platter. "Oh? Then they're upstairs. Call them, will you—dinner's almost ready."

I went upstairs and checked both rooms. No boys. I came back down just as they came in the front door. "Where've you two been?"

"Next door."

"Sybil's?"

They nodded and headed for the television set.

"Whoa, wait a minute. Dinner's ready, come on." They sauntered past me toward the dining room. "Let's see your hands."

"Oh, Dad," Eddie groaned, "Mom already made us wash them when we came home from school."

"Hands," I said firmly. They held them out. "Then where did all the chalk dust come from? Soap and water in the downstairs john. Make it snappy, I'm hungry." Unenthusiastically, they went.

I turned back to the kitchen just in time to be handed a potato masher.

"What's wrong with the electric mixer?"

"You always say it makes them mushy. Come on, start thumping."

As I drained the water from the potatoes I asked, "Did they tell you about their I.Q. tests?"

Liz looked up from the stove. "No," she said questioningly. "Bad news?"

"Depends on how you look at it, I suppose." I told her about my meeting with Headley.

"A hundred and *seventy?*"

"Makes you think, doesn't it?"

"Oh, Ray—they won't be fit to live with. Do they know?"

"I'm not sure. I'll broach it gently at dinner."

I waited till we were having dessert. "Ran into your history master at the British Museum today," I said casually.

"Old Deadly Headley?" Eddie said. "What was he doing, crawling out of a mummy case?"

Richard giggled at this bold display of irreverence. I pretended not to notice. "He told me you two had taken I.Q. tests, that right?"

Eddie nodded, shoveling chocolate cream pie. "Lot of stupid questions. I had to give up games period."

"How did you make out?" I asked. Liz caught my eye and we waited for the answer.

"Aw, he said we did pretty good."

"What's pretty good?"

"I don't know. He said we passed, so it's okay. Hey, Mom, can I have another piece of chocolate pie?"

"Please," Liz said.

"Please," they both chimed. Liz gave me a secret smile and went to get it. Just then the phone rang. A minute later Liz popped her head around the door. "For you," she said, her tone accusative. I went out. "It's a man named Monroe. From Sotheby's. About the table. Ray—you're not going to sell it?"

Damn him, I thought. He said he'd send a *written* report. "No, Liz, I'm not. I'll explain later." I picked up the phone.

"Ah, Mr. Armacost—do forgive me for ringing like this, but I've just made a rather interesting discovery and I thought you might like to know."

"Oh?" I said, and waited. Liz was standing watching me.

"Well, I've checked this very thoroughly and unless I'm terribly mistaken your table is genuine late fifteenth-century Florentine. Early Renaissance."

"Yes, I had been told it might be," I said. Liz frowned, puzzled by this one-sided conversation. She moved a little closer, trying to hear. I pressed the receiver hard against my ear to keep his voice from leaking out.

"Ah, but that isn't all. There was a maker's mark. Difficult to trace, but I've managed to come up with some extremely interesting information. It seems that a table by this maker was ordered by Pope Sixtus the Fourth and was sent to the Papal Nuncio in England to be presented to Richard the Third when he assumed the crown. It is quite possible that this table is the one in your possession."

"Well, that is interesting," I said, trying to sound very unconcerned. "You wouldn't like to hazard a guess as to how much it might bring at auction?"

Liz caught her breath and gave me a betrayed look. I shook my head quickly to let her know the question was purely academic.

"Oh, dear me, sir—this is always a difficult question. But I would hazard a guess and say that, properly advertised, it would fetch in the neighborhood of, hmmm—forty to fifty thousand guineas."

I wasn't sure I'd heard him right. "Fourteen to fifteen hundred?"

He chuckled. "Dear me, no, Mr. Armacost. I said *forty* to *fifty* thousand—it might even fetch more."

I tried not to show any reaction for Liz to see. I swallowed, feeling almost faint. Monroe went on, "Were you thinking of putting it up for auction?"

"I'd have to give it some thought."

"I understand. But if you should decide, we would be pleased to handle it for you. In the meantime I will prepare a written report and send it along in a few days."

I hung up. Liz, glancing toward the dining room to make sure the boys were not listening, whispered, "That's five hundred more than Gilpatrick! Oh, Ray—you're not thinking of selling it?"

"Of course not," I said around a mouthful of cotton. I was trying to figure out how much fifty thousand guineas amounted to in dollars. My brain wouldn't function, but at a rough guess I knew it was more than a hundred thousand.

"We'll talk about it later."

We did. In my study, after the boys were safely upstairs in bed. Liz was a trifle cool as she sat down beside my desk. "You still don't trust Sybil, do you. You just had to have a second opinion."

"I trust her less now than before."

"Why? Her Mr. Gilpatrick said it was *only* a guess when he said it might be worth a thousand. So the other man said maybe five hundred more. They're both *estimates*. It doesn't detract from the fact that Sybil was making an honest effort to help."

"She was making some kind of an effort all right," I said. "Just how honest is another story. Claremont Gilpatrick is as phony as a three-dollar bill! Oh, there is a Claremont Gilpatrick all right, but that guy Sybil sent this morning wasn't he. I checked with Sotheby's and found out that Claremont Gilpatrick is in Germany—*was* in Germany the morning Sybil's fat friend showed up here.

"And another thing—that estimate . . ." I stopped. Something *made* me stop. It scared me. In all our married life Liz and I had never kept anything from each other. But for some reason I just could not bring myself to tell her that the table the boys had bought for twenty pounds was worth a small fortune.

I wonder now, looking back, if it would have changed things if I had.

But she was too concerned about Sybil to notice what I had been saying. "No!" she said firmly. "I just know there must be some explanation. She wouldn't do a thing like that."

"Well, it seems that she has."

"But why, Ray? What would she get out of it—half of a five-guinea fee?"

"I don't know why she did it," I said. "The point is, she

did. And I don't like it." But I was beginning to wonder how long it might be before Sybil would try to buy that table. Or send somebody along to buy it for her.

Liz got up slowly, looking like a child who has just been told there is no Santa Claus. "I just don't understand." She turned to look at me. "Ray, will you promise me one thing?"

"What?"

"Promise you won't say anything to her. Not yet, anyway. Not with our anniversary dinner tomorrow night and that spinet and everything."

Ah, the spinet! No wonder Sybil could afford to give away antique spinets. "No, of course I won't say anything, Liz. Do you think I'd just run over and collar her and ask who that phony character was?"

"You might—if you got mad enough."

"Well, I'm not mad enough. Not yet. But I don't like it, Liz. I just don't like it. And—speaking of promises—I want you to promise something, too."

"Yes?"

"Don't go over and tip her off. Don't tell her I've found out about Gilpatrick or it will give her a chance to cook up some excuse."

"I promise. I wish I hadn't planned that damn dinner for tomorrow night. It's going to be absolute hell trying to act normal."

It was, too. We were not exactly in a party mood when we rang her doorbell the following evening at seven. Sybil made a great fuss of kissing us both and wishing us a happy anniversary. It was downright embarrassing. She went on chattering as she showed us into her gloomy overstuffed sitting room with its hodgepodge of Victoriana and musty smell.

"Bunting isn't here yet," she said, bustling over a tray of bottles and glasses, "but he won't be long."

The boys stared longingly at the TV set, the only twentieth-century item in the room apart from the dangling electric chandelier which was almost in the antique category itself. They looked at me and the message was plain but I shook my head. Sybil caught the drift.

"Would you boys rather watch television? Yes, I'm sure you would—you don't want to sit and listen to the old folks chatter on. Why don't you go up to the back bedroom and watch on the portable. You know where it is." The boys nodded and shot out of the room.

"Are you sure it's all right?" I asked. I didn't like the idea of them barging around somebody else's house, especially one with so many knickknacks. For budding geniuses they could be pretty damn rough sometimes.

"Don't give it a thought," Sybil said. "They're perfect angels every time they come here."

Liz tried to brighten the gloom by developing this into conversation. "Yes, isn't it strange how much better behaved your children seem to be in somebody else's home?"

"Oh, forgive me, Liz, darling, but I've just remembered!" She clasped her hands coyly, giggling. "You must have thought I was a silly girl!"

"Why, Sybil—what's wrong?" Liz asked.

"Gilpatrick, of course!" Liz and I exchanged quick glances.

"What about him?" I asked.

"I'm so glad I found out before you discovered anything was wrong or you might have thought, goodness knows *what* you might have thought."

"Thought what, Sybil?" I said.

"Why, my darlings, the man who came to value your table wasn't Claremont Gilpatrick at all. Of course, I didn't *see* him so I didn't know until this morning when I had a letter from Claremont, apologizing. He had to go to Germany, quite unexpectedly at the last minute, to view some glass—it's his specialty, you know, though he does know a lot about all sorts of antiques—and he asked a friend of his to come in his place."

I looked at Liz. "But—I thought you said . . . yes, you did. When you called me out of the study you said Gilpatrick was here."

"I took it for granted. When I answered the door he just said he'd come to value the table. So naturally I took it that he was Gilpatrick."

Sybil giggled. "Of course you would, my dear. Now, how about little drinkies all around, eh? I've some very nice homemade wine. . . ."

While she rattled on I went back over the morning "Gilpatrick" had arrived. Come to think of it, neither Liz nor I had called him by name. And he hadn't bothered to give his own name or to explain. He was not the kind to bother with social niceties. Then something hit me.

"The check!" I said out loud.

Liz and Sybil looked at me. "What check?" Sybil asked.

"You made it out, Liz. Whose name did you write on it?"

"Why—Claremont Gilpatrick, of course. I didn't dream . . ."

"It doesn't matter," Sybil said. "Claremont will reimburse him. Now, Ray—try some of this. It's a special of mine. Herb and berry wine. I think you'll like it." She handed the glasses around and Liz and I relaxed a little now that the explanation had cleared the air. As to the vast difference in the two estimates—well, it was obvious that Sybil's man, while he had some knowledge of antiques, lacked that special bit of insight that made Monroe the expert he was. And the difference between being able to value an ordinary antique and the expertise to discover a rarity was about a hundred thousand dollars.

The doorbell rang just then and Sybil put down her glass. "That'll be Bunting." Watching her go, all flighty and trivial, I wondered how I could have seriously taken her for anything other than a frivolous middle-aged woman, good-natured and bumblingly well-intentioned.

Liz looked across at me and pulled a triumphant face.

I raised my glass with a silly grin by way of apology and she returned the toast. We both sipped. "Pooh!" Liz said, spluttering. I gasped, feeling it burn its way down into my stomach, leaving a bitter taste like alum on my tongue. It was ghastly.

Liz poured hers surreptitiously into one of the potted plants on the table beside her. I looked at the liquid in my glass. It was difficult to see what color it was because the glass itself was a vicious green and so was the decanter Sybil had poured it from. I rose to pour mine after Liz's just as Sybil came back in with Father Bunting. I stood holding the drink and looking guilty while hellos were said all round and Father Bunting wished Liz and me a happy anniversary.

"George, some wine?" Sybil asked, approaching Bunting with decanter and glass.

"Thank you, no, my dear. You know I seldom drink on an empty stomach."

"But this is a special occasion. Married fourteen years, isn't it sweet? Just look at them. So young. You'd never believe it."

"I'm sure they won't hold it against me if I toast them abstemiously," Bunting said. "My good wishes are none the less sincere for their lack of liquidity."

Sybil laughed. "Have you ever seen him at a loss for words? The Jesuit training, you know. Liz, my dear, your glass is empty." She moved toward her with the decanter threatening. Liz placed a protective hand over her glass. I smiled as she tried to wriggle out.

"Thank you, Sybil. It was delicious. I love homemade wine, but I'm afraid it's a bit strong for me. Goes straight to my head."

"Which is the general idea, darling," Sybil said, removing her hand with playful firmness. "If you can't get a little bit tiddly celebrating your wedding anniversary what's the point in living?"

I watched in smug amusement, holding my scarcely touched glass while Liz was treated to a refill. Sybil turned on me. "Ray? Oh, come on—look at you! You've barely touched it!"

"I'm a slow starter. I'll catch up."

"Now I'm not having that. Pour that down and let me give you a refill before I go out to the kitchen. How can we have a convivial evening if you're all going teetotal on me?"

"No, honestly, Sybil, I . . ."

She looked hurt. "You don't like it."

"No, really—it's great. Only . . ."

Liz drove the nail. "Oh, come on, Ray, don't be a spoilsport!"

Cornered. I gave Liz a frozen smile, took a breath, and swallowed the wine. It went down like liquid fire, a cross between vodka and thousand-octane napalm flavored with old boiled sagebrush roots and powdered alum. I felt my lips begin to pucker. Through the tears in my eyes I could see Liz grinning. Sybil refilled the glass. I could smell the fumes of the stuff rising like something from out of the Pit.

It must have been powerful stuff for I don't remember much of what happened before and during dinner. I wasn't exactly drunk, I just didn't register everything that was going on. I remember another earnest discussion with Father Bunting about good and evil. I could see his face come into focus occasionally and then recede. I remember seeing Liz take one or two sips of her wine and then pour it into the plant pot while Bunting's back was to her. You louse, I thought, leaving me to do all the dirty work! But, and this was strangest of all, I remember reaching for the decanter voluntarily, not once but several times, and wondering why I was doing it.

Dinner was a nothingness with a haze of floating faces and a buzz of conversation. I found myself thinking I *must* be drunk, yet surprisingly my movements were fairly steady; I ate mechanically and conversed automatically with very little recollection of what I ate or what I said. Once I caught Liz looking at me oddly. Then Sybil poured her a glass of wine and because there were no plant pots on the dining table, she had to drink it, a sip at a time, dragging it out through the meal.

After dinner Liz excused herself to go to the bathroom. I remember that much because I was thinking I should go there myself. She came back looking a little white but smiling and I excused myself and went down the hall to where I thought the downstairs toilet should be. I opened one door which disclosed a cupboard filled with brooms and mops. I tried another and found a room almost devoid of furniture, uncarpeted, with something standing in the center of the room. I tried the light switch but nothing happened. In the dim light from the hall behind me I saw a curved line chalked at my feet and remember thinking that Sybil must have marked the floor where the carpet should go. I closed the door and went out. The next door I tried was the right one. One thing I remember distinctly. I poked my finger down my throat and made myself vomit. The toilet bowl filled with a horrible green mess.

My next recollection was of sitting in my study, feeling dizzy, a pile of typed notes in front of me on the desk in a dazzling pool of light while the rest of the room was in shadow. I undid my tie.

Liz came in wearing her nightdress and housecoat, her face floating white against the dark. "Ray? Are you all right?"

"I won't be long. Go on to bed, I'll come right up." She started to go, giving me an anxious backward glance.

"Liz?"

"Yes?"

"Was I drunk?"

She seemed uncertain. "I don't know. You were *something*. And you looked peculiar. But your speech was normal. I think it was that wine. You had quite a lot. I threw mine up."

"So did I. Awful stuff, wasn't it?"

"You'd better come to bed."

"Be up in a minute."

She nodded and went out, closing the door. I sat for a minute, wondering what the hell I was doing there. I couldn't read my notes. Nor was I really interested. I felt as though a huge chunk had fallen out of my brain leaving a void. For a moment I felt a twinge of alarm and wondered if I would ever be all right again. Then I decided that it was only the wine and it was time I got up to bed and slept it off.

I stood up to go and found myself weaving. With an inebriate's fumbling precision I tried to shuffle my notes into a tidy pile, then moved the *Southwind* papers parallel to the edge of my desk. A place for everything, I thought, and gave a slightly drunken giggle. I paused to riffle through the *Southwind* papers, wondering if my brain would ever clear sufficiently to make sense of them again. Then something caught my eye. I leaned against the desk to steady myself and turned back a few pages. There, staring up at me, was something I hadn't noticed when I'd gone through them before. A print from an old woodcut. The portrait of a man in Elizabethan dress. "Captain Sir James Tyrell," the cutline read. The fumes of the wine receded, and there was a moment of cold, clear sobriety in which I felt as though ice water suddenly had been released inside my belly. The face seemed to be staring at me, trying to tell me something.

Giddiness returned and I swayed slightly, clutching at the desk for support with a clumsy movement that sent the papers cascading to the floor. Carefully I bent down and gathered them up, trying to keep my balance as I straightened. I fell back into the chair, then laid the papers on the desk and made a fumbling attempt to sort through them in an effort to find the picture. But the dizziness was on me again and after a minute I gave up. I would go through them in the sober light of morning.

I got unsteadily to my feet, feeling slightly nauseated. The room smelled musty, like Sybil's house. Full of herb-like odors. It must have been that weird wine still fuming in my head. I thought I had better open the window and let the study air out overnight. I swayed to the window, fumbled open the catch, and tugged at the sash. It stuck. I tugged again and it suddenly gave way, shooting upward with a clatter as a gusty draft whipped into the room and sent my typed notes flying like feathers in a storm. One sheet fluttered on the windowsill and as I made a grab for it, it slipped over the edge into the darkness of the patio.

To hell with it, I'd find it in the morning. I went to the door, surprised at the rubbery condition of my legs. By the time I reached the foot of the hall stairs I had an attack of conscience about the sheet of paper lying out there on the patio. I had no idea what was on it, but it might well be the result of a whole week's work. I couldn't risk losing it. I went down the hall at an unsteady gait and took the flashlight from the alcove, then started back down the hall toward the patio.

The hall began to extend as though made of rubber, like some kind of passage in a house of horrors at an amusement park. I found myself swaying, bumping the walls on either side. My vision was growing more blurred and I was afraid I was going to pass out.

The sudden rush of night air when I stepped out onto the patio revived me a little. I shined the light around and located the sheet of paper on a rosebush near the top of the wall between our place and Sybil's. It was too high for me to reach so I picked up a garden chair and carried it unsteadily to the foot of the wall. As I heaved myself up onto the chair something told me that I had better be quick about it, my strength was ebbing fast. I felt sleepy, dizzy.

I plucked the paper from the rose thorn and was about to step down when something caught my eye—something that penetrated even my semicatatonic state. From the top of the wall I looked down onto the back window of one of Sybil's downstairs rooms. A shaft of dim yellow light was coming through a chink in the heavy curtains. I could hear the faint sound, eerie, like voices chanting. Shadows moved across the curtain in rhythmic succession as though in some sort of dance. Someone brushed against the curtains and they parted still further. What I saw then, although it was floating in my vision like an underwater scene, made me sure I must be losing my mind.

The room I recognized, vaguely, as the one I had peered into by mistake earlier in the evening. The curved line of chalk I had seen was now fully revealed as part of a complete circle chalked on the board floor of the room. The object in the center of the room was a small table covered in black velvet. On it was a human skull with two crossed bones. The only light came from a single black candle stuck to the top of the skull. Around this peculiar altar four persons were dancing, holding hands, and chanting as they circled the skull. They were Sybil, Father Bunting, Eddie, and Richard. They were all stark naked. I felt myself slipping into blackness as deep and soft as the velvet beneath the skull. I remembered nothing more.

6

I REGAINED CONSCIOUSNESS LYING IN MY OWN BED STARING
at the ceiling. At first I could see only the blinding white
glare of reflected sunlight on the white plaster and I was
afraid I had injured my optic nerves in some way. The
back of my head was one agonizing ache and each
pulsebeat seemed to expand and contract my skull with
such pressure that I could feel the jagged ends of bones
grating together. Or so it felt.

"Ray?"

I dropped my eyes from the ceiling and found myself
staring straight into Sybil's face. She was sitting beside
my bed in a yellow silk dress, her hands folded calmly in

her lap. In a flash I contrasted this with the last time I had seen her, stark naked, her huge breasts bobbing and swaying, fat hips shuddering as she pranced in the candlelight.

"How do you feel?" She was smiling as though nothing had happened.

"Where is Liz?"

"Out shopping. She'll be back in about an hour."

She was lying. I knew she was lying. "Where are the boys?"

"At school. The doctor said you were all right so we saw no need to keep them home." She leaned closer, still smiling, and laid a hand on my arm. "You had a nasty fall, darling. How much do you remember?"

I swallowed, trying hard to think of a convincing lie. The agony of concentration was unbearable. "Not much," I managed to say.

"I think it was probably my fault. I shouldn't have let you drink so much of that homemade wine. It is fairly powerful."

How much did she know? Was she aware that I had seen their witches' sabbat over the garden wall?

"Did you say I fell?"

Sybil nodded. "Liz said you were in your study about midnight going over some notes. She thought you were a bit tight, but she was too tired to argue so she went up to bed. Apparently you started to follow a few minutes later but didn't quite manage. You must have passed out going up the stairs and struck your head on the newel-post when you fell."

There was something wrong here. I could remember that I had been standing on the garden chair when I began to black out. Had I really made it inside and started up the stairs?

"Liz found me?"

"No, she was sound asleep. I think she must have had a little too much wine, too. One of the boys heard the thump and got out of bed. He tried to wake Liz but couldn't, so he came over and rang my bell and got me out of bed. Bunting and I came over and carried you up here and then phoned the doctor."

"Father Bunting?"

Her expression changed for an instant. "Yes. He sometimes stays the night in my spare room." She smiled and tried to pass it off lightly, but I had a feeling that she had made a slip of the tongue. If only I could talk to Liz and see how much she knew about all this. I was convinced that the wine had been drugged to insure that we would be sound asleep when the sabbat began. I wondered also if it might not have contained an amnesiac so that we wouldn't remember anything if we had wakened. This theory would account for the blank patches in my memory during the early part of the evening.

My head was pounding from the exertion of thinking. I closed my eyes. "That's right," Sybil said soothingly. "Have a good sleep and you'll feel better."

I nodded feebly to show that I had heard, but I felt no desire for sleep. As far as I could rationalize the situation in my present confused state, two explanations presented themselves. The first one—and the one that circumstances increasingly led me to believe must be the right one—was that some force, I could only call it Evil, had entered our lives. And, somehow, that force was connected with this woman who called herself Sybil Rodne. Also, the Italian table in the downstairs hall had some bearing on the situation. But by far the most frightening aspect of this whole business was the fact that, if all the foregoing were true, then this woman had exerted some kind of diabolical influence over our two sons. For what reason she might want to do this, I could not even begin to comprehend. Yet I felt that their innocence and her evil were drawn together as irrevocably as the opposite poles of a magnet.

The second explanation was that I myself could be suffering from some obsessive complex brought on by a succession of strange experiences which, individually, might be nothing more than the product of a writer's overactive imagination, but which collectively added up in my mind to frightening reality. This latter explanation, disturbing though it might be to me personally, was infinitely preferable. Once recognized, it could be cured, perhaps by simple rationalization, or if it persisted, then perhaps by some medical or psychiatric treatment.

As I lay with my eyes closed, withdrawn into my own little shell of private torment, I earnestly prayed that the second of these alternatives might be the true case. For if it were not, where was I to turn to combat the threat that seemed destined to destroy the innocence of our two little boys? If I went to the police with my present evidence they would consider me nothing more than a crank and I couldn't really blame them. Who else was there to turn to?

After a few minutes I heard the rustle of silk and the soft closing of the door as Sybil left the room. I opened my eyes a slit to make sure she had gone, then when I saw the room was empty I opened them wide. The bedside telephone was on the nightstand within easy reach. I wanted desperately to call somebody. Anybody. Just to establish contact with reality. Liz was out shopping, so Sybil had said. There was no way I could check on that. But I could find out if the boys were really at school. I raised myself on my elbow and winced as the throbbing threatened to burst my skull. I waited a minute for it to subside, then picked up the phone.

I didn't know the number of St. Bartholomew's and the directories were down in my study so I did it the hard way, first dialing the operator to ask the number for information, then dialing "directory inquiries" to ask the number of the school. When I finally got through a familiar male voice answered.

"Who is that?" I asked, keeping my voice low in case Sybil might be listening in the hall.

It was Peter Headley.

I was glad it was not Henniker-Harnsworth. I explained to Headley that I had slipped on the stairs and suffered a slight concussion. "I was just phoning to let the boys know I've regained consciousness and feel fine." I hesitated, wondering if the next question might sound as though I were checking up on them. I phrased it carefully. "They haven't been too upset, have they? I mean, do they seem to be their usual selves?"

"Oh, yes, perfectly normal. I've just seen them in the refectory—at least it hasn't affected their appetites."

I hung up feeling relieved. Temporarily, at least. It is amazing how quickly a note of normalcy abates panic. But I was far from feeling that everything was all right. Quite the contrary. *If* Sybil was an instrument of evil—whatever that might mean—she was also very clever. Clever enough not to proceed if she thought I might be the least bit suspicious. She would wait until the apparent return to a sane state of affairs had once more lulled me into complacency. It takes a very short time for one to forget a nightmare when one awakes to familiar surroundings.

The door opened again and Sybil returned carrying a glass on a tray. "Everything all right, Ray?" she asked cheerfully. "I thought I heard you talking as I came up the stairs. Were you calling me?"

"I phoned the school to see how the boys are, that's all."

An uneasy look seemed to flit across her face but it was gone in a flash. She smiled and held out the glass. "That was very thoughtful of you. They were worried about you when they left. Here, drink this. It'll help your head."

I looked at the glass. It was filled with a grayish-white liquid. "What is it, emulsion paint?"

Sybil laughed. "No, it's a special concoction from my herb garden."

My reaction was plain on my face and Sybil laughed again. "You silly boy—it's a prescription the doctor left. Now come on, drink it."

I took the glass and held it for a minute. I had no recollection of any doctor and I had only her word that one had been called. "I don't like taking drugs unless they are absolutely necessary," I said firmly and put the glass on the bedside table.

"Very well, have it your own way." She reached for the glass but I beat her to it. "No, leave it," I said. "Maybe I'll have it later."

Sybil glanced at the chiming clock on the mantelpiece, then checked it against her wristwatch. "Bunting will be here shortly to help me bring over the spinet."

I put my hand tentatively to the back of my head and encountered a bandage. "What's this for?"

"You cut your head slightly when you fell. Nothing serious, just a couple of stitches."

"Oh, Lord—if I got blood on the stair carpet Liz'll kill me."

"There wasn't much blood. Just a little on your hair. Certainly none got on the carpet, thank God."

(111)

The doorbell rang downstairs and Sybil jumped up. "That will be Bunting. I'll go down and let him in." She went out, leaving the door open. I waited until I heard her on the stairs, then I leaned out of bed and grabbed her handbag and opened it. I had only a few seconds. Already I could hear the priest's voice as she opened the door and greeted him. Aside from cigarettes, lighter, key ring, a lace-edged handkerchief, and the usual cosmetics, there was nothing out of the ordinary. Then in the mirror pocket I found a snapshot. It was a picture of Sybil and Father Bunting standing beside the lych-gate of a country church. I turned it over. On the back was written with a ball-point pen, "All Hallows Church, Elhamstead." I put it back and closed the handbag just as I heard them coming up the stairs.

Father Bunting looked concerned as he came in. "My dear boy, how do you feel?"

I wanted to tell him that I would feel a lot better when he and Sybil were behind bars. Instead I said, "Not too bad, thanks, Father. Nice of you to drop by."

Sybil said, "Before I put you to work, George, perhaps you and Ray would like a cup of tea?"

"I was hoping you might suggest that," he beamed. "And a thin slice of bread and butter wouldn't go amiss. That is, if I might impose on Ray's hospitality. I'm afraid I missed lunch at Farm Street. I've been at the British Museum all morning and lost all track of time. When I finally got back it was too late."

"How about some bacon and eggs or something?" I suggested. "As long as you don't ask me to join you."

"Bless you, that would be lovely," Father Bunting said.

This was a stroke of luck. It would get rid of Sybil for

at least twenty minutes, time that I could put to good use quizzing Bunting without her being around to hear what was said.

"How's the head?" he asked when she had gone.

"Better now," I told him. "But I won't be able to stand on it for at least a week."

He laughed. "You had a nasty fall. All due to Sybil's overgenerosity with her homemade wine."

"I notice you didn't touch it," I said pointedly.

"Not on your life. I've had it before. One learns circumspection as one grows older. How is the writing coming along?"

"All right, up until now." I switched the subject. "Father, do you recall our conversation that day we met at the British Museum? You said you wondered if any of us really realizes his own potential for good or evil, and you said something about there being a delicate balance that could be tipped one way or the other without our being able to do anything about it."

Was that a guarded look in his eyes? His answer was offhand. "Vaguely, yes. Why?"

"Oh, I don't know. I suppose it appealed to me as a writer. There might be something there worth exploring. Particularly in connection with the motivation of characters."

"Yes, I dare say," he replied without enthusiasm. He did not seem anxious to pursue the point. Getting up from his chair he went to the window and looked down onto the patio. "I suppose this crack on the head will retard your research for a while, eh?"

Was it a casual question, or was he trying to find out something? "I suppose so," I said. "I don't feel like poring over ancient manuscripts in my present state if that's what you mean. Anyway, I've got plenty of notes downstairs to keep me busy as soon as I feel like working again."

"Ah, that's good," he said, turning with a smile. "There's nothing worse than being a recuperative invalid when you'd like to be getting on with some work."

I was determined to return to our previous subject and I felt he was trying to avoid it. "You said something else the night you were here—something about the Devil being very necessary, because without evil there could be no good."

He turned away from the window abruptly and went back to his chair, saying, "Did I? Yes, perhaps I did—to the annoyance of some of your other guests, I'm afraid."

Was he reluctant to come back to the subject, or was this abruptness because he was afraid I was going to start an argument just as Charles Sealey had? I decided to clear the air on that point, so I apologized for Sealey's behavior. Bunting took it in good grace. "My dear boy, you mustn't feel you have to apologize for other people. As a priest I'm quite accustomed to these rather pointless, unprovoked attacks. It seems sometimes that men like Sealey use them as some sort of a defense mechanism. They are disturbed because they have no belief of their own so they feel they must attack someone else's. Thereby hoping to prove, I suppose, that if the believer puts up an adequate defense of his belief it automatically proves that the attacker is justified in not believing. Which overlooks the very fundamental point that faith cannot ultimately be rationalized or it would not then be faith."

I felt he was very cleverly evading my own attack by drawing the line of discussion into other channels. So I came back abruptly to what I was driving at. "But I'm interested in what you said about no good without evil. Again, from the standpoint of a writer. I can glimpse just a little of what I think you mean by it. At first glance it seems like a contradiction in terms, or at least a very confusing philosophical view."

Now that I had pinned him down to the subject a strange calm seemed to take over. He lit a cigarette, not nervously, but with a casual movement, blowing smoke contemplatively toward the ceiling. It was the action of a man who felt complete confidence in what he was about to say. I could feel it like a physical reality in the room. It was as though I had at last tuned in to his wavelength. But I was not at all certain I was going to understand what he would say. In this, to a certain extent, I was right.

"Perhaps it is paradoxical," he began quietly, "but like most great truths it is basically very simple. Yet because of this very simplicity it is most likely to be misunderstood, if not completely discounted. The difficulty with philosophical discussion—or theological discussion for that matter—is that people are so absorbed in the complexity of life that they expect the solution to its problems to be equally complex, when in reality it is usually quite simple. And so it is with this understanding of the necessity for the coexistence of good and evil. The explanation is so simple as to be almost incomprehensible, unless one strives to understand."

"So far, Father," I said, "I am completely confused. Perhaps that's because I don't understand simplicity. You say there is a necessity for the coexistence of good and evil. Then why does your church teach that evil is an undesirable thing and should be eradicated?"

He smiled. "Your question proves what I have just said. The complexity of simplicity. But let me try to give you an illustration. It is one of the basic laws of physics that for every action in nature there is an equal and opposite reaction, right?"

"I was never any good at physics," I said, "but I seem to have heard something like that."

"Well, it's a very essential part of natural law. Without it there would be chaos. For instance, the wind blows against a tree at so many miles per hour, and the tree offers resistance with equal force."

"But sometimes trees blow down," I said.

"In which case the force with which the tree falls is resisted by the earth with equal force. So what you have envisaged as a hole in the theory actually becomes its proof. Take it a step further and consider modern space flight. The action is the backward flow of gas and the reaction is the forward thrust of the rocket."

"So for every evil act there is also a good act—is that it?"

"Now you are treading on very thin philosophical ice. In theory, yes, otherwise there would be chaos just as there would be chaos in the physical world if the law of equal and opposite reaction were abrogated. But if you mean that the act of a man striking his neighbor in London is offset by another man doing good for *his* neighbor in San Francisco, then I'm afraid we have to leave such minute tabulations to Almighty God. But in theory, yes."

"Then are you saying that evil is necessary because it is the force that creates its opposite reaction, namely good?"

"Before I do that, I must make it quite clear, Ray, that this is strictly *my* opinion and not the dogma of the Roman Catholic Church, though it may not be in disagreement with the opinion of certain theologians within the Church. Do you understand?"

I couldn't see what all the fuss was about and I said so. "After all, I just want your opinion. Not even necessarily as a priest. More as a"—I found it hard to say the word—"friend."

"Then the answer is yes. Evil is necessary because it activates its opposite force, good."

He was looking at me strangely when he said it, his eyes staring vacantly as though not even aware of my presence. He seemed to be contemplating something that was in the room with us but beyond my physical vision. It gave me a strange feeling.

"Would it follow that a thoroughly evil person, provided there is such a thing, would feel it his—his *duty* to perpetrate evil in order to bring about good?"

He blinked his eyes and I could see them focus once more on my own. Whatever had claimed his attention for that brief moment was gone. But his voice, when he answered my question, now sounded very tired, very old, as though he were suddenly drained of energy. "An evil person," he said slowly, "—and there is such a thing, believe me—would feel it his duty to perpetrate evil whenever possible. But not for such a laudable motive."

"But you just said that evil was necessary because it brought a counteracting good!"

"And I pointed out the danger of oversimplification for just this reason. In the system of counterbalances which exists in the universe—ebb and flow, action and reaction, light and dark, good and evil—we discover only the law, not the motive. You see, Ray, in the beginning there was nothing *but* good. Then along came that angelic shop steward, Lucifer, who decided he could organize things and make good even better. In other words he was out to satisfy his own desires, which by their very nature—

because they opposed the existing good—were evil. So his *motive*, like that of every evil person who has followed since, is not to perpetrate evil in order to bring about good, but an attempt to conquer for his own ends."

I had my answer. And a very frightening one it was, too. I was convinced that the man seated before me, dressed as a priest, professing to be a priest, had just revealed his true self to me. My fear was now for my little boys. I had no idea how I could combat what was going on. I had no real notion even of what *was* going on. I only knew that there was a force of Evil walking the face of the earth, and I felt that a dedicated convert to the ultimate aim of triumphing over Good sat with me in this room. From now on I must tread warily, for the last thing I wanted Father Bunting to realize was that this was more than a casual discussion.

We could hear Sybil humming merrily as she came up the stairs. Bunting got to his feet, moving heavily, like a person weary to the point of exhaustion. "You see, Ray, those who are evil feel that their objective is the only one worth fighting for, even as those dedicated to the cause of goodness feel the same about theirs." He turned to face the door as it opened and Sybil came in breezily, balancing a tray of bacon and eggs, toast, marmalade, a pot of tea, and three cups.

"What have you boys been talking about?" Her questioning eyes met Bunting's.

He gave a little laugh. "I'm afraid we were deep in philosophy and theology."

"Oh, dear! Ray *will* have a headache now. Where would you like to sit? Here—next to the window where you can get the sun. We may not have much sunshine from now on. It's nearly November. All the darkest months lie ahead."

Bunting laid his napkin across his lap. "Yes," he said wearily, "indeed they do."

Liz came home twenty minutes later. She popped upstairs for a few minutes to see how I was, then she and Sybil and Father Bunting went next door for the spinet. I heard them bringing it into the downstairs hall, moving things around in the drawing room to make a place for it. Finally, I heard Sybil and Father Bunting leave.

I quickly debated how much I should tell Liz right away. Already she had given me queer looks because of my attitude toward Sybil and the table—an attitude that I felt was now more justified than ever. Perhaps it would be best to let everything lie quiet for a day or two until I got on my feet again. Then I could do a little detective work. Just what, though, I wasn't quite sure. But I wanted to come up with something that would prove to Liz that I didn't have a kink someplace or that I hadn't gone loony from the fall on my head. Also, each time before when I had broached the business of Sybil and the table, the answer had always seemed to come a little too pat. It was as though Sybil were psychic and could anticipate my moves before I made them. Just how to combat *that* I wasn't sure either. Stop thinking, I supposed.

"Hi, how do you feel?" She smiled, sat on the bed, and gave me a kiss. I held her close, the feel of her reassuring after what I had just been through. Again I almost fell for that sensation of security that comes with the slightest return to normalcy—the awakening after the nightmare. I was beginning to think again that I had been unduly suspicious of a garrulous middle-aged woman and a harmless priest. This time however it was going to be different. I was not going to gush out my theories and have them derided. I would bide my time, provide some sort of evidence, then act. Meanwhile I would keep a very close watch on the boys.

"Liz, how drunk was I last night?"

"Not very. That's the funny thing, Ray. At least I don't *think* you were. You asked me the same question when I talked to you in the study before I went to bed. Remember?"

"Vaguely. I was going over my notes, wasn't I?"

Liz nodded. "How much do you remember of what happened?"

That seemed a strange question coming from her. Had Sybil put her up to it, I wondered. Innocently, of course. "Not much," I said truthfully. "I felt more tired than drunk, yet my legs got wobbly and I have a very hazy recollection of the whole evening."

She lay her head on my chest. "I'm glad you said that. I thought it was just me. I couldn't remember much, either. Yet I wasn't drunk, I know that. I didn't have nearly as much as you. Must be powerful stuff, that homemade wine of hers." She sat up. "Want anything to eat?"

"I might manage some soup. My stomach still feels queasy."

"Okay, I'll make you some soup and toast," she said, straightening the bedspread and tidying the bedside table. She noticed the glass with Sybil's emulsion paint. "You didn't drink your medicine!"

"I'm not taking any more drinks Sybil offers me."

"You nut! It's not something she brought over—it's the prescription the doctor left."

She picked up the glass. "And you talk about the way the boys behave when *they're* sick. You're the biggest baby of the bunch."

"Liz?"

She turned. "Yes?"

"I was just thinking—it's funny that the boys heard me fall. They're both usually such sound sleepers. Instead it was you who slept through it."

"That wine again. They couldn't even wake me."

"Did I do any damage?"

"Not even a dent in the newel-post."

"No blood on the stair carpet?"

"Fortunately for you, no."

"Who finally woke you up?"

"Sybil. She came upstairs and I went down and helped them carry you up. Now do you want soup and toast or are you going to keep me standing here talking all afternoon?"

She opened the door.

"Liz . . . Do me a favor, will you? Bring me up the *Southwind* papers. They're on my desk in a manila folder."

"Oh, Ray—you're not well enough to start working. Can't you let it . . ."

"No work, I promise. I just want to check something, that's all."

In a few minutes she was back with the folder. "This it?" she asked, laying it on the bed.

"Yes—thanks."

She went downstairs and as I began shuffling through the papers I could hear muffled domestic noises from the kitchen. I got through the folder once without finding the portrait. I went through again, very carefully this time, feeling each sheet to see if there might be two stuck together. Still no portrait. There was a flaw here some-where. I just might have dreamed that part about finding the portrait and chasing one of my notes out into the gar-den. I remembered feeling dizzy as I stood up from my desk. Did I open the window, or had I really tried to go straight upstairs to bed and passed out? Surely I would have remembered *something* about it.

And yet—there *were* other blanks in the evening. The first thing I would have to do when I got on my feet would be to look through my notes and see if any of the sheets showed signs of having been impaled on a rose thorn. Could I have dreamed that? And the dancing around the skull by candlelight? No. *No*, by God. This time I wasn't going to let myself be talked out of anything.

I sat up. My head thumped and threatened to split. I shut my eyes and waited for the pain to subside. Then I steadied myself on the arm of the chair and stood up. The room swayed a little before settling down. I went gingerly to the window and looked down onto the patio. The wrought-iron garden furniture was all in its usual place. But then someone could have put the chair back after I had fallen.

The distinctive click of the pop-up toaster came faintly up the stairs. Liz would be coming in a few minutes. I turned away from the window and was easing my way toward the bed when I caught sight of a crumpled scrap of paper in the chair where Father Bunting had been sitting. My head was pounding furiously now from the exertion but I hung on long enough to grab the piece of paper before falling back into bed. I slid it under the pillow and lay back with my heart and head both pounding as Liz came into the room.

"Letter for you," she said and put it in my hand. She

was clearing a space for the tray on the bedside table when she saw my face. "Ray, are you all right? You've been out of bed, haven't you?"

"I had to go to the john."

"Oh." She spread a table napkin and put the tray on my lap. "Aren't you going to open it?"

I fumbled the seal and unfolded the letter. "It's from Sotheby's valuer. Confirming what he said about the table." There were a couple of other paragraphs reiterating his speculation as to its antiquity. My head was thumping too much to read them. I put the letter in the envelope and laid it on the bedside table and began eating my soup.

"Hold it!" She picked up a glass and held it out to me. "Your medicine, remember?"

I drank it. My first estimate had been correct. It tasted exactly like emulsion paint. I hurried back to the soup to kill the taste.

"Will you be all right on your own if I leave you for a couple more hours?" Liz asked.

"Sure. Just lock the front door. I don't want any visitors, just a nice long sleep. Where are you going?"

"I heard Ralph Nelson is in London putting together a new picture. I thought I might go and say hello, and just ask if he knows of anybody who's looking for a script-writer."

"What if the boys come home while you're gone? I don't feel like pounding down the stairs to open the door."

"They won't be home till four thirty. I'll leave a note on the door to tell them to go over to Sybil's till I get back so they won't disturb you."

"No, don't do that!"

"Why not?"

"Because I—I don't like to take advantage of people's

good nature. The boys are over there too much lately. It's an imposition."

"Sybil doesn't mind. She loves them."

"I still think they ought to come home. Leave the door unlocked. I'll keep an ear open in case of burglars."

"Fat chance of your hearing anything, but it's too late now. That medicine has a sedative to make you sleep."

"Then we'll have to risk it. But I don't want the boys bothering Sybil."

We left it at that. I finished my soup and toast and she took the tray downstairs. She came back a few minutes later, changed dresses, fussed with her face, kissed me good-bye, and left. I was feeling sleepy as the medicine began to take effect. When I heard the front door close I took the wad of paper from beneath my pillow and unrolled it. It was a form notice from the manuscript department of the British Museum telling Father Bunting that a certain manuscript would be reserved for him the following Monday as requested. I wadded up the paper and flipped it to the wastebasket beside Liz's dressing table. It missed and rolled underneath. Sleep began to take over; my head felt light, painless. I slid deeper under the blanket and let myself sink blissfully into the valley of oblivion. In the final twilight that separates consciousness from sleep I thought I heard the front door open quietly, but I wasn't sure. I was too drowsy to care. Somewhere in my dream I heard the distant tapping of typewriter keys.

7

I DIDN'T WAKEN UNTIL THE FOLLOWING MORNING, SATurday. My head was only slightly sore, the throbbing had gone. I had a ravenous appetite. At breakfast Liz broke the news that she had all but signed a contract with an English producer who was looking for someone to write a treatment on the life of Nelson. Not Ralph, Horatio. She had promised to take the boys to see Windsor Castle as a celebration. It was meant to be a family outing if I felt well enough, but I declined saying I had too much work to do.

It was a beautiful October day: clear, crisp, and sunny. Liz packed a picnic lunch and I waved them off from the front steps.

The patio room was warm in the autumn sunshine. Lulled into complacency by the weather, I walked over to the white wrought-iron garden chairs. There was a muddy footprint on one of them, more obvious because someone had tried to wipe it off and hadn't completely succeeded. Also, there was dirt on one of the legs.

I squatted and examined the soft ground of the rose beds next to the wall that separated our garden from Sybil's. The imprint of a wrought-iron chair leg was just where I thought it would be. That would account for the dirt on the leg of the chair that also had the footprint. I went back and got the chair and brought it over and placed it near the wall so that the leg fitted exactly into the imprint. Then I stood on the chair and looked over the wall.

I found myself looking straight down into Sybil's astonished face.

"Ray! What on earth are you doing?"

"I was just thinking about pruning these roses," I muttered stupidly.

"You silly boy—I pruned them for you yesterday! Didn't Liz tell you?"

"No. She must have forgotten. I'm afraid neither of us is much good as a gardener. I couldn't even tell they'd been pruned."

I got down feeling like a complete jackass. Anybody with two eyes could see that the roses had been pruned almost to nothing. Before I put the chair back, I had a good look at the paving stones. If I had fallen and cracked my head badly enough to need stitches, surely there would be some blood somewhere. There was no blood. But there was a clean patch on one of the flagstones, as though somebody had recently washed it. I put the chair back and went inside.

Back in my study I leafed through the pile of typewritten *Southwind* notes that was still on my desk. My memory of that evening was too hazy to remember any particular thing I might have been reading, so I went through them all looking for one that looked muddied or rumpled or gave any indication that it might have been impaled on a rose thorn. Nothing. I shuffled them together and was about to lay them aside when I noticed something. The edges of one sheet were slightly irregular. I pulled it out.

The typing was from my own typewriter, I could tell that by the characteristic jump of the out-of-line letter *a*. But the edge of the sheet looked as though it had been inexpertly cut with a razor blade. I held it up to the light and compared it with one of my own. The two papers had different watermarks.

The irregularity of the strange sheet puzzled me for a minute until I realized that since coming to London I had habitually ordered my paper cut to the old standard American size, 8½ x 11 inches, because I found the English A-4 size too large. So whoever had inserted this strange sheet had cut it down from a larger one. There was one telltale clue. Whoever had copied my notes—for I was certain that was what happened—had overlooked an obvious point. In transcribing my notes on *Southwind*'s visit to Port of Spain he or she had automatically reverted to the English spelling "harbour" instead of the American "harbor." So the typist had not been Liz.

The conclusion seemed obvious. I *had* chased one of the sheets of paper out into the garden that night. Possibly it had become muddied, or even bloodied, or torn on the rosebush when I fell—and somebody was trying to cover up by substituting a copy. The object being, of course, to destroy positive proof that I had gone out of the house that night so that any recollection I might have of a witches' sabbat over the garden wall could be laughed off as "too much wine."

Then I remembered hearing the typewriter as I drifted off to sleep the previous afternoon. Sybil. She had seen Liz leave and, knowing that I would be drugged from the medicine, had slipped into the house and retyped the sheet on my own typewriter. And, not knowing where I might keep my typing paper, she had come prepared with a sheet of her own. Only it wasn't until she had finished typing and started to put the page back in with the rest that she found it was a different size. Rather than retype the whole thing she had cut it down to size.

I shoved the notes aside and lit a cigarette. The time had come for serious contemplation of what was going on around me, or perhaps more correctly, what seemed to me to be going on. The evidence I had gathered so far was, I had to face it, negligible. Everything could be explained away by coincidence, misunderstanding, alcoholic delusion, or just plain overactive imagination. But deep inside me I could *feel* that something was wrong. I knew it wasn't just my mind.

I have always thought of myself as a normal, healthy human being, and like most people I am extremely skeptical about any happening that cannot be rationally explained. So it was very difficult for me to sit at a desk in normal surroundings in the heart of a busy twentieth-century metropolis and seriously contemplate that my sons were being influenced by witchcraft. For that was what it seemed to boil down to. Witchcraft. Moreover, what purpose could be served by such behavior was completely beyond my comprehension. What could Sybil, and Bunting too if he were involved—and I felt sure he was—possibly hope to gain by influencing two young boys? Father Bunting. Suddenly I remembered something.

I stubbed out my cigarette and ran upstairs to the bedroom where I dropped on my knees beside Liz's dressing table and groped for the ball of paper I had tossed there yesterday. It was still there. I opened it and read it again, particularly the identity of the manuscript that Bunting had reserved. There was no title, only the reference number, *Add. MSS* 36674, which meant it was something from the collection of Additional Manuscripts in the British Museum. I shoved the paper in my pocket and phoned for a taxi from the bedside extension. Ten minutes later I was on my way.

I paid off the taxi in the forecourt and ran up the steps between the huge granite columns and through the revolving doors. Pushing my way through the Saturday crowd of tourists I went straight to the Manuscript Room, showed my card to the guard, and went in. I found a seat, made out a request slip for *Add. MSS* 36674, and sat down to wait. A few minutes later an attendant came up.

"Mr. Armacost?"

"Yes."

"I'm afraid that the document you want is in a volume that is being rebound at the moment. It won't be available until Monday, but even then I'm afraid we have a reservation for it. If you could come back next Tuesday we could hold it in reserve for you."

I considered this for a moment. Tuesday was three whole days away. "A friend suggested I check this manuscript. Is there any way I can find out what it contains?"

"The catalogue of Additional Manuscripts will give you some idea of the subject matter."

She led me to the section of bound catalogues lining the walls and found the place for me. Additional Manuscript No. 36674, I read, was the *grimoire* of a witch—a handbook of black magic—which belonged to the sixteenth-century scholar Dr. John Caius. I closed the catalogue. So Father Bunting was busy doing his homework.

I left the Manuscript Room and went into the Reading Room where I ransacked the general index for books on witchcraft and black magic.

That afternoon was a revelation. I had gone in a skeptic. I had emerged several hours later under a cloud of gloom, convinced—as nearly as any skeptic can be convinced—that such things as witchcraft and black magic did exist. Father Bunting was absolutely right. Somewhere in the world there was a force of Ultimate Evil. But then—he should know.

It was nearly dark when I paid off the taxi at the front door and let myself in. Liz was on the hall phone. She gave me a glance which was a combination of annoyance and relief and said into the mouthpiece, "He's just come in, Doctor."

She hung up, relief winning over annoyance. "I was worried stiff."

"Sorry. I thought I'd be back before you or I would have left a note." I held her away from me and glanced upstairs. "Liz, I've got to talk to you. Let's go where the boys can't hear us."

She turned away toward the drawing room. "Well, let's talk over a drink. I could certainly use one. And don't worry about the boys overhearing—they've gone away for the weekend."

"Gone for the weekend? Where?"

"Someplace in Sussex. Sybil has a married sister there. She rented a car and Father Bunting drove them down."

I nearly dropped the gin bottle. "My God, Liz!" I grabbed her. "*Where?* The name of the town! We've got to get them back!"

"Ray—don't, you're hurting me!"

I released her and she pulled away, rubbing her arm and looking at me strangely. "Liz—I'm sorry. But you've got to *understand.* The boys are in danger and I'm not just making something up. I've spent this whole afternoon looking through reference books—Sybil is a witch, I'm sure of it. And Bunting—he may not even be a priest—is what they call a witch's 'familiar.' They're working on the boys, I'm sure of it. They . . ."

I stopped. From the expression on her face it was clear that I was not getting through. To her, I was babbling nonsense. I tried a calmer approach. "Liz, trust me. We can't afford to take chances. Already two men, John Dighton and Miles Forest, both connected with our boys, have come to grief. Dighton is dead, Forest barely escaped. I will try to explain everything on the way down to Sussex. I'll go get the car and you be ready when I get back—and for God's sake try to remember the name of the town. I promise you I am *not* crazy—I know what I'm talking about. Just trust me, that's all."

I bolted out of the house and ran across the now darkened square and around the corner to the garage in the mews. I backed the car out with a squeal and a roar and skidded around the square to our place. Liz was waiting on the curb. She got in looking pale, hugging her coat about her in the chill evening air, and giving me an uneasy glance.

"Ray, don't you think we ought to go in and talk this . . ."

"Liz, *please!* We'll talk on the way down." I rummaged in the glove compartment for the map book and switched on the top light. "Sussex, Sussex," I muttered, thumbing through the pages. "East or West Sussex?"

"She just said Sussex."

"What was the name of the town?"

"Ray, I honestly don't know."

I groaned. "Oh, my God. Liz, *think!* Didn't she give any kind of a name? Any place they might be going to see over the weekend?"

"Well . . ." Liz chewed her lip. "She said there were one or two old castles—or were they abbeys?—they wanted to show the boys. And they said something about the Battle of Hastings."

I flipped to the map index and found Hastings. "It has a castle," I said. "And there's another down the coast a few miles at Pevensey, and—here's another a few miles inland at a place called Bodiham." I gave her a hopeful look. "Any of those ring a bell?"

She shook her head. "I sort of got the impression it would be a village or a small town where her sister lived. It wasn't Hastings, but it had something to do with the Battle of Hastings. You know, where William the Conqueror . . . Oh, I wish I had paid more attention."

"I wish you had damn well kept the boys at home!"

"Ray, that's not fair!" She was on the verge of anger. "I don't see why you're making all this fuss. All these ideas about witches and . . ."

"All right, all right," I said gently, trying to calm her. "Let's just see if we can find the place and I'll *explain*." I started down the index alphabetically, reading out place names.

"Aldbourne?"

"No."

"Alceston, Aldingbourne, Alfriston, Amberly . . . ?"

"I don't think it began with an A."

"Balcombe, Barcombe, Barlavington . . ."

Liz said, "Give me the map and let me look."

"Wait a minute—we're wasting time sitting here—just let me see how to get out of London on the road for Hastings. Then you can look for the name of the place as we drive along." I memorized the general direction, handed the map to Liz, and gunned the car out of the square, heading for the Embankment and Westminster Bridge.

"Here it is!" Liz said suddenly. "Battle."

"You sure?"

"Positive. I remember thinking what a bellicose name for a peaceful English village."

Fortunately there was little traffic at this time on a Saturday night. It was the lull between commuters going home to suburbia and the swingers coming out for the nightlife. I put my foot down along the Embankment and the speedometer crept up to sixty. I prayed that the Metropolitan Police had other things to keep them busy. As we swung up the approach to Westminster Bridge, Liz asked cautiously, "Ray—how are you going to find where her sister lives?"

"When we get down to Sussex we'll look in the phone book and . . ." I stopped and glanced at her. "Don't tell me you don't know her sister's name?"

"Why should I? She just said they were going to stay with her sister and her husband. You never think to ask people the name of their married sister."

"We'll find them," I said grimly. "I'm not giving up till I do."

"Ray—I'm scared."

"By God so am I!"

"No—you don't understand. I'm afraid—well . . . You've got to admit you've been acting strangely lately. Don't you think you're . . . maybe . . . overreacting?"

"Now, honey, just listen for a minute," I said in my most reasonable voice. "I know I've said some things about Sybil that have seemed unfounded. But this time I'm convinced that I'm right. There are too many things that can't be explained."

"Such as?"

"Remember when you found me in the study Thursday night—I was going over my notes, wasn't I?"

"Yes."

"And you went on up to bed and the next thing you knew Sybil was waking you up to tell you I'd fallen on the stairs and hit my head on the newel-post."

"That's right."

"Well, I don't think it happened that way at all. After you went upstairs I felt stuffy and a little dizzy. So I got up and opened the window." Then I told her about going out onto the patio to look for the sheet of paper. When I described what I saw when I looked over the garden wall Liz stared at me openmouthed.

"Ray, for God's sake! Sybil and Father Bunting . . . stark naked? Dancing around a . . . ?" She was too amazed to speak. "You were dreaming!" she gasped finally. "The boys had gone to bed hours before. But to think Sybil and Bunting . . ." She started to laugh. "The mind boggles!"

"Did you *see* the boys go to bed?"

She stopped laughing. "Why—no. But they were in their pajamas when I woke up."

"But you don't remember whether they left Sybil's and

went home to bed of their own accord? You don't remember looking in their bedrooms when we came home to
see if they were there?"

She was no longer laughing. "I don't remember. But I
know they wouldn't do a thing like that." She fell quiet.

"I'll tell you something else. You know how Sybil fools
around growing a lot of weird plants? Well, I found out
this afternoon that there are all kinds of herbs and things
that are used in witchcraft and black magic. Some modern
medicines are derived from them. But in the hands of
some unscrupulous person . . . Take that wine, for instance. I'm sure it contained an amnesiac. Something to
make us forget."

"Ray, don't—you're not making sense. You don't think
you *really* saw them. Dancing. The boys?"

"Liz, right now I don't know what the hell to think. But
I know that we were both sick that night and vomited part
of the wine. That would decrease the effectiveness of the
amnesiac, but it wouldn't destroy it completely. You had
less than I, so your memory is probably better. But it
made you dopey and you went to sleep. Now I swear I
chased that paper out onto the patio that night. And yesterday after you'd gone I thought I heard my typewriter
being used. When I went into the study this morning I
found somebody had come in and retyped one of my
notes. The sheet that I . . ."

"Oh, Ray—that was Sybil!" Liz said, breathing relief.
"When we picked you up from the bottom of the stairs
you were clutching this piece of paper—sort of crumpling
it in your fist. I saw it was one of your notes and said
you'd have to retype it and Sybil said she would come
over and do it since I was going out yesterday anyway."

"No, Liz. It's too pat. Every time something happens

there's always an answer. And the answer is always just a little too convenient. Why should she offer to type my notes?"

"She only offered to do it after I suggested it needed to be retyped."

"Which was all very convenient for her. Liz, stop and think. Did that sheet of paper have any dirt on it—as if it might have blown around the patio? Or did it have a tear or a hole in it where it might have caught on a rosebush?"

"Oh, Ray, I don't know. I wasn't concerned about a damn piece of paper right then. I was worried about you."

"Exactly. So think back. Was it really *you* who made the first remark about the thing needing to be retyped—or was it Sybil?"

"I don't remember."

"Well then I'll tell you. It was Sybil. I'll bet anything you want. Because I had a sheet of paper in my hand when I passed out. But I didn't pass out *inside* the house. I fell off the chair in the patio and they either saw me or heard me fall, came over, and carried me inside to make it look as though . . ."

"You're talking about your own *sons*—not just Sybil and Bunting!" She sounded horrified.

"Damn it, I'm trying to *tell* you. They are under the influence of these two fiends." She was shaking her head as I went on. "That sheet of paper could have been proof that I had fallen outside on the patio, so Sybil put the idea into your head that it needed to be retyped. She took it, didn't she—so that you wouldn't get a chance to see it?"

Liz was very quiet for a minute. "Ray, I simply don't believe, influence or no influence, that our boys, *our own sons*, could be conniving in this . . . this business. Why, I

(136)

saw them—standing there in their pajamas, looking as worried as could be about you."

"But you've got to admit that there is something strange going on. I'm not saying that Eddie and Richard are doing this willingly. These people, whatever they are, have somehow managed to get control over our boys. I don't know how, I only know that it's happened. And we've got to get them away from them."

"Ray, just tell me one thing. Why? Why would anyone do anything like that to two innocent boys?"

"Because there is such a thing as evil, just as Bunting said. And by God, he should be an expert. I looked up one of his reference works at the British Museum this afternoon, and do you know what it was? A sixteenth-century witch's handbook—a guide to black magic."

We were into the outer London suburbs now and rolling toward Bromley. Liz was quiet for a long time, watching the anonymous houses flash by, lighted homes with ordinary people going about the business of an ordinary Saturday night. I wondered what they would think if they knew the mission that was sending us past their doorsteps in the night.

"Oh, Ray, I don't believe it," Liz said at last. "These things just don't happen. Some people had us over for a wedding-anniversary dinner, you got tight on homemade wine, and cracked your head when you slipped on the stairs. No. I simply don't believe all this sinister business. You dreamed that you saw Sybil and Bunting and—and the boys—dancing like that. It's a typical Freudian dream. Everybody has dreams like that. Ludicrous situations where quite respectable people you know are cavorting about naked."

"Then why did Sybil come over yesterday and prune those roses? Out of neighborly kindness, or just to make sure any evidence of my having stood on a garden chair to look over the wall might be covered up? And why did she wash a patch of paving on the patio? To wash up the blood where I cracked my head."

"Wrong again. She dropped a bottle of stuff she was spraying on the rose beds to keep greenflies from propagating in the spring."

"Very convenient!"

"Ray, you're being unreasonable. In the first place it just doesn't make sense. This is the twentieth century. There is no such thing as witchcraft."

"Then why is it you keep reading about black-magic rites in the Sunday papers?"

"Because there are queer sorts of people who like to have an excuse to cavort around and hold orgies. Just as they smoke pot or go in for transcendental meditation. Just to be doing something different. But do you honestly believe that ordinary people can gain control over another person's—*soul?* And make them do what they want them to do? Do you honestly?"

I had to consider that for awhile. "Liz, I don't know. All I know is that something is happening. I can *feel* it and I'm worried. Worried about what it might be doing to our boys." She said nothing but I could tell she wasn't convinced.

We remained silent for a long time. It started to rain as we drove over the North Downs, and by the time we crossed the Medway south of Sevenoaks the rain had become a downpour. Each of us was silent with his own gloomy thoughts—and doubts.

It was Liz who finally broke the silence. "Ray, if we get

there tonight and find there is nothing wrong, will you promise me something?"

"Depends on what it is," I said cautiously.

"I think you ought to see a psychiatrist."

There it was. I had been expecting it so it didn't upset me. But I didn't want to tell Liz that I had already contemplated that step myself as a possible alternative. "*If* we find nothing is wrong," I said.

I knew that when we found Sybil and Bunting—*if* we found them—the circumstances would speak for themselves.

"By the way," I said, "Keep your eyes open for a roadside phone booth."

"Who on earth are you going to call?"

"I'm not sure. Probably the police, for a start. But I think I'll call a couple of car-rental firms in London and see if I can get the number of Sybil's car. You don't happen to know where she got it, do you?"

"I saw the sticker on the windshield when I was saying good-bye to the boys. I've seen it before—a big white letter R in a blue circle. But I can't think of the name."

I found an Automobile Association phone booth beside the A21 just outside of Pembury and pulled onto the shoulder. Once inside I phoned the local AA office and asked for the name of the car-rental agency with the blue and white R insignia.

"Yes, sir, here it is. The Regency Car Hire Service." He gave me a phone number in Knightsbridge and I dailed it.

"Regency Car Hire."

"Hello—I'm trying to locate a neighbor who hired one of your cars this afternoon. Her mother has suddenly been taken ill and we don't know how to contact the daughter.

Her name is Sybil Rodne. Can you give me any idea of where she might have gone?" I felt I had to lie or he might not want to give out the information. Even then he hedged.

"We don't usually divulge information about clients, sir."

"Look. Shall I call the police and have them ring you?"

"That won't be necessary, sir. What was the lady's name again?"

"Sybil Rodne. R-O-D-N-E. No Y. Can you give me any idea where she might have gone?"

I could hear the rustle of pages, then a pause. "Hello, sir—yes, we have a Mrs. Rodne, but I'm afraid she didn't give any indication of where she was going. I mean, people don't always say, do they?"

"Can you give me the number and make of the car? Maybe I can get the police to help."

"Blue Vauxhall Viva. Registration LRU 487 S."

I wrote it down, thanked him, and went back to the car.

"I've got the number of the car. Take a look at the map and see what's the next town of any size."

"There isn't any big town till we get to Hastings. Why, what are you going to do?"

"Go to the police and ask them for help."

"And tell them what? That our boys have been kidnapped by witches?"

"Give me credit for some sense, Liz. I could tell them the same story I just gave the car-rental people—that Sybil's mother is ill and that we're trying to locate Sybil."

"And if they locate her first and tell her that her mother is ill, then what? I don't even know if her mother's still alive. And if she finds out you're behind it how are you going to explain? We're going to look damn silly, aren't we? How are you going to explain our arrival without arousing Sybil's suspicions?"

"I don't really care about Sybil's suspicions or what she thinks just so we get the boys back all right. Anyhow, we could just say that I felt like taking a rest from work and that we decided to do a little castle-hunting ourselves."

"I still think it's going to look strange," Liz insisted.

"Then I'll think of something else. But just let's find them first."

"It would cause all kinds of complications to go to the police at this stage. You know how thorough they are. They'd want to know the address of Sybil's non-ill and possibly non-existent mother, and when they found you were fibbing they'd want to know why. I think we'd better try something else."

I looked at my watch. It was nearly seven thirty. The rain had stopped and the clouds had been swept away over the South Downs leaving an expanse of bright moonlight. The countryside was gently rolling, with tiny hamlets tucked away in wooded pockets in the valleys. I had a sudden inspiration.

"Liz, how big is this place Battle?"

She checked the map with a flashlight. "Just over four thousand."

"Good, that makes it easier."

"I don't understand."

"Well, it isn't a very big place. It shouldn't take us long to cruise around and locate a blue Viva with a license number LRU 487 S."

"Suppose it's in a garage?"

"The chances are it won't be. In a small place how

many people have garage space for more than one car? Visitors usually leave theirs standing outside or in the drive."

"Suppose the sister doesn't live right in the village? We can't spend all night driving around the countryside."

"Then we'll have to go to the police."

"Well, I've got a better idea," Liz said firmly. "But right now you'd better slow down because we're coming into Battle. Let's stop at the first pub we come to. Maybe we can pick up some local insight."

We parked in a lot at the rear and went inside the bar marked "Lounge." It was still too early for the Saturday-night crush and we found seats at the bar without trouble. The place was the kind you wish there were more of; old beams and gleaming brass, with antique guns and swords on the walls. The landlady came over, all smiles, and I ordered two dry martinis.

"Americans?" she asked pleasantly as she served the drinks.

We admitted we were and she said the same thing we had heard a hundred other places from Oxford to Canterbury, "We get quite a few Americans through here. Mostly in the summer, though."

"We're not tourists," Liz said brightly. "We live here—I mean, in London, that is. As a matter of fact we're trying to locate a good friend of ours. She's visiting her sister here in Battle but we're stuck because we don't know the sister's married name. Isn't it silly?"

"Perhaps I can help you. My husband has lived here most of his life and knows everyone within twenty miles. What is the name of the lady who is visiting here?"

"Sybil Rodne," Liz told her. We held our breath.

The landlady's brows puckered. "It doesn't ring a bell."

She called her husband who was in conversation with a couple at the other end of the bar. "Peter, have you ever heard of anyone around here called Sybil Rodne?"

Peter came over rubbing his brow. "Rodne, Rodne. Now hang on a tick, something's stirring. Live around here?"

"No," I said, "but her sister does. But we don't know the sister's name."

The man at the end of the bar spoke up. "Peter, isn't that the name of the woman who gave a lecture to the garden club about six months ago? She had a sister somewhere near here." He came over. "Would this Missus Rodne be a funny old duck who . . . I beg your pardon, no offense intended if she's a friend of yours!" He looked embarrassed.

We laughed. "Well, you could call Sybil a funny old duck," Liz said.

"Well, if it's the one I think it is she talked to the garden club about growing herbs and that sort of thing."

"That's the one!" Liz and I almost shouted.

"Ah, I remember now!" Peter boomed. "Mrs. Marlwood's sister. Yes, of course. You know her, Doll," he said to his wife. "She had you cooking dandelions and nettles and God-knows-what for a while. Said they were chock-a-block with vitamins and you were shoveling them at me for about a month till I threatened to leave home unless you went back to cabbage and sprouts."

Everybody laughed. Liz and I managed a polite smile. Then I asked where this Mrs. Marlwood lived. Peter put a pad on the bar and drew a crude map. "Colonel and Mrs. Marlwood, Clavicula Cottage, that's the place. You go out of here toward Battle Abbey . . ."

I thanked them for their help by ordering a round of

drinks from which Liz and I excused ourselves by saying we were in a bit of a hurry. Back in the car I gave her a squeeze and a congratulatory kiss. Now that we were so close there was, I think even in Liz, a growing fear of what we might find. For my part I couldn't keep my mind from flashing back headlines from the Sunday tabloids about ritual murders and weird cults like the Charles Manson thing in California. My God, I found myself thinking, these things really *do* happen.

As we turned down the lane marked on the landlord's map Liz turned to me. "What *are* we going to say?"

"That you had a phone call from a producer friend from the States who happened to be in Hastings looking it over as a possible location. Somebody told him we were in London, so he rang up and we drove down for a quick drink and a quick chat."

"Why didn't we stop on the way down?"

"An appointment to keep—didn't have time. And it wasn't until we were coming back through Battle that it dawned on us that this was where *they* were, so we thought we'd drop in and say hello. Okay?"

Liz nodded.

"Hang on, we're here." I swung the car up the hedge-lined drive. Sure enough, there was a blue Viva with a reflective number plate beaming LRU 487 S.

It was a picturesque cottage standing in a field on its own without a neighbor in sight. Crooked walls and half-timbering, painted black and white with a charming olde-worlde garden that must have been a delight in the summer. As we stepped out of the car in the moonlight we got a breathtaking view of the distant sea beyond the south-ward slope of the Downs.

Someone heard our car and a pair of carriage lamps beside the door came electrically alive. A woman about Sybil's age came out onto the thatched and honeysuckled tiny front porch.

"Mrs. Marlwood?"

"Yes," she said, with that note of half-suspicion you give to someone who knows your name when you don't know his.

"We're the Armacosts. Edward's and Richard's mother and father. Sybil's next-door neighbors from London."

Her face lit up. "Oh, how delightful!" She held out her arms to embrace Liz. "Do come in—Sybil will be delighted."

We were ushered into an extremely pleasant and, for a cottage, surprisingly large room with low, beamed ceilings, an inglenook fireplace with a cheerful log fire, chintzy curtains, wing-backed armchairs, and lots of old brass and copper. In one of the chairs, facing us, Father Bunting looked up from a chessboard. The occupant of the other chair was hidden from view, but seated on a low stool watching the game were Eddie and Richard. They accepted our arrival with the aplomb of youth, and went back to watching the game.

Bunting pushed back his chair and rose, beaming. "Well, this is a pleasant surprise!"

Sybil came from the kitchen wiping her hands on an apron. "Liz! Ray! How delightful to see you!" She came over and kissed Liz and said, "Well, well!" A tall man with iron-gray hair and military bearing came in and Sybil began the introductions. First Nancy Marlwood. The tall military-looking man was Colonel Roger Marlwood, Nancy's husband.

Sybil then turned to introduce us to the man who had been playing chess with Father Bunting and who had now risen from his chair. "I don't think you've met . . ." Sybil began.

"Sir James!" I said in astonishment.

He came forward, hand outstretched. "Hallo, old chap! What a remarkable coincidence! But then I should have guessed it as soon as I met these two lads. Striking resemblance." I introduced him to Liz.

"Where did you two meet?" Father Bunting asked.

"Same place as you and I, George," Sir James told him. "Public Record Office, snooping through musty documents."

"How on earth did you find us?" Sybil asked.

I told of our fictitious visit to the producer in Hastings and they all seemed to accept it as perfectly normal. Drinks were poured and everybody relaxed. Everybody, that is, except me. I couldn't get it out of my mind that once again everything seemed to work out too neatly in Sybil's favor. But I had to admit that the circumstances seemed innocent enough.

Liz gave me a smile over the rim of her gin and tonic as much as to say, "So this is your witches' coven, eh?"

"Tomorrow we're going down to Pevensey to see the castle," Eddie announced.

"We'll all go together, now that your parents are here," Sybil said as though she really was pleased we had come.

"Oh, no!" Liz said apologetically. "We'll just finish our drinks and go."

Sybil turned to me. "At least say you'll stay for dinner."

"Of course they will," Nancy said resolutely. I didn't need a second urging and neither, really, did Liz.

Nancy and Sybil came in bearing dishes. I scrutinized them warily, fearing some of Sybil's herbalistic concoctions. But I needn't have worried, it was a roast brace of pheasants with all the trimmings. It was a feast by any standard, enhanced by the glow of candlelight on silver and flickering shadows among the beams of the low ceiling.

"How does this champagne compare with my home-made wine, Ray?" Sybil called down the table.

Roger Marlwood looked up sharply. "My God, you didn't drink any of that stuff, did you? Wonder you're still alive!"

Everybody laughed.

The conversation continued in a similar vein all through the meal, light banter interspersed with comments about where they had been that day and where they planned to go tomorrow. It was all so damned normal that I felt the old sensation of guilt beginning to creep back. And with it came the niggling worry that I might really be developing some sort of psychosis. But before I was willing to accept that theory I needed a hell of a lot of convincing.

Bunting and Sir James were talking chess, some involved discussion about "the Caro-Kahn defense." It went completely over my head, but Eddie and Richard seemed to be listening with interest. They had never shown any interest in chess before—probably because they hadn't been introduced to it—but already I was beginning to accept the fact that such staggeringly high I.Q.'s would probably lead them to learn the intricacies of chess as other children might learn ticktacktoe.

I waited for a break in the conversation and then spoke to Bunting. "I meant to tell you, Father—you dropped a slip of paper when you came to visit me the other day. I don't think it was important—a notice that they've reserved some manuscript or other for you at the British Museum."

"Very kind of you, Ray, but no, I won't need it. They'll hold it for me anyway." He turned to Roger Marlwood. "Incidentally, Roger, this will interest you. I've come across a sixteenth-century *grimoire* at the B.M. If you like I'll make a transcript and send it to you."

"What on earth's a *grimoire?*" Nancy wanted to know.

"It's a sort of witch's grammar, isn't it?" Sir James put in.

"Oh, he's not interested in things like that anymore!" Nancy said. "That was *two* hobbies ago. Before that it was chess. Then came fishing—which took him away from home too much—and then Father George got him interested in black magic. Or was it you, Sybil?"

"I didn't know you two were interested in black magic," I said innocently, looking straight at Sybil and then at Bunting.

"Only as a subject for discussion," Sybil said blandly. "Would you care for more potatoes, Liz?"

After a fattening dessert of Black Forest gateau we retired to the living room for coffee and before we knew it the grandfather clock was clanging eleven and the boys were up way past their bedtime. Nancy and Liz saw them upstairs to bed, then Liz and I said our good-byes and thank-yous and started for London.

"Well?" Liz said as we drove through the winding hedgerows back toward Battle.

"Did you notice the way she dodged the question of black magic?"

"She didn't dodge it, she simply stated that they were interested in it only as a subject for discussion. If they had been trying to dodge anything Father Bunting wouldn't have mentioned that he had found that—what did he call it?—that witches' handbook, now would he?"

"That was only to allay suspicion in case I had gone and checked on the manuscript."

"You're being melodramatic."

We were quiet for a while, nursing our own thoughts. The moon was now in full brilliance over the South Downs, the floating white clouds like bolls of cotton pinned to a dark blue velvet curtain.

Liz stretched, yawned, then snuggled down in the seat. "What a heavenly night. If there was anything to your witchcraft theory they wouldn't be sitting around a family fireside playing chess on *this* particular night. It's Halloween."

Instinctively I slowed the car. From what I had read that afternoon at the British Museum I knew there were four times of the year that were important festivals in the witch's calendar. February Eve, May Eve, August Eve, and—November Eve. Halloween.

Liz sat up and looked at me. "For God's sake, Ray, you're not taking me seriously?"

"The thought had occurred to me," I said.

"Ray, can you honestly imagine—can you visualize"—she ticked them off her fingers—"Sir James Tyrell, Nancy and Roger, Sybil and Bunting, Eddie and Richard—all traipsing stark naked into some rain-sodden field on a frosty night to dance by the light of the moon after feasting on pheasant and champagne?"

I drove on. Liz sighed and snuggled down again. But all the same I wished we had insisted that the boys come home with us. I shouldn't have left them under the same roof with Sybil and Bunting until I had resolved this business one way or the other.

"Ray?" Liz murmured sleepily. "Will you do what you said you would?"

"What's that?"

"You said that if we found the boys and everything was all right you would go see a psychiatrist. You promised."

I gave in. Just to keep the peace. Or so I told myself.

"Okay. I'll phone for an appointment Monday morning."

8

IT WAS WELL PAST MIDNIGHT WHEN WE ROLLED THROUGH sleeping London. There was almost no traffic now. As we drove along the Embankment, the Thames lay sheet silver in the moonlight. There was a sparkle of frost on the grass as we turned into Bentley Square.

I stopped the car in front of the house and shook Liz awake. She raised her head and stared sleepily out of the window.

"Home, sweet home," I said. "Hop inside and get ready for bed. I'll put the car away."

She sat looking at the house standing white in the silent moonlight. "Ray—the house looks strange. Drive around to the garage. We can walk back together. The cold air will make me feel better."

I drove around the square and down the mews to the garage. Liz got out while I put the car away. She was standing there hugging her coat around her and shivering when I came out and locked the garage door. We started to walk down the mews.

"Cold?"

"Freezing."

But I knew it wasn't just a frosty night. Liz is a warm-blooded animal.

We turned into the square and cut across, the grass crunching slightly under our feet. It was quiet. So quiet that when we crossed the pavement Liz's heels tapped in loud echoes from the surrounding houses. Our shadows fell ahead of us, sharp and clear.

I saw it then. A third shadow. Standing there beside our own. I glanced around on both sides. We were the only two people on the square. But the shadow remained. It had no real shape, but it was not formless. It was distinct, clear etched. Like our own.

I urged Liz toward the steps. "Do you see the shadow?" I asked. The words came out of their own volition.

"Ray, it's a trick of moonlight, a reflection or something." She was wrong but I didn't want to frighten her. I fished for my key, trying to keep my voice light and my hand from trembling. "Of course you're right. You put the coffee on and I'll go up and turn on the electric blanket." I pushed open the door and reached around the jamb for the hall light switch. The light was reassuring, warm, welcoming. Liz went in quickly and I followed and shut the door.

I took Liz's coat and hung it with mine in the hall closet while she went into the kitchen. Then I looked at the table—cherubs. I went up to the bedroom and switched on the electric blanket. As I was turning to leave I caught sight of the letter from Monroe at Sotheby's still lying on the bedside table. I put it in my pocket, intending to read it over my coffee.

As I stepped out of the bedroom into the hall I heard a strange noise.

It wasn't Liz. I could hear her making the coffee downstairs. I started down the stairs and the noise came again. From somewhere *upstairs*. I tiptoed back onto the landing and listened. It seemed to be coming from above the ceiling. I looked up. There was a tiny trapdoor high above the landing. I had never been up there but I knew it was an access to the loft where, I had been told, resided some mystery of English plumbing known as "the tank." By now I had grown used to its occasional groanings and gurglings, but this sound had been different. A dragging, shuffling noise. Soft, but distinct. Rats?

I listened for another full minute but the sound was not repeated. With a shrug I started downstairs. Jitters. They are contagious.

"I made cocoa," Liz said when I came into the kitchen. "I thought coffee might keep us awake."

I didn't mention the noise. We sipped our cocoa and our eyes met across the rims of the earthenware mugs. "What was that noise, Ray?" So she had heard it too.

"You know what I think? I think we've got a ghost." She was dead serious. "This house is haunted, Ray. It's got nothing to do with Sybil or the boys or anything like that. I've never really believed in ghosts—but I've never really *not* believed in them, either. But this is England and—well, you know how the English are about their ghosts. All the best old houses have them."

"Then we'd better move."

She put her cup down and shook her head, wiping the brown cocoa crescent from her upper lip with a paper napkin. "Nope. If a ghost is a restless spirit then perhaps we ought to try to help. They usually *want* help, I've read. That's why they come back."

"I don't know. But Father Bunting will. Don't they have exorcism in the Catholic Church? You know, pray for the soul of whoever it is and tell the ghost to go rest in peace—that kind of thing."

I was ready to go along with her. But only part way. Maybe we did have a ghost. But I was firmly convinced we had far more on our hands than just a spirit from the past. And I did not want to mention this one to Father Bunting.

We left it at that. Liz rinsed the cups while I checked that the doors were locked. She was in her dressing gown and brushing her teeth when I came into the upstairs bathroom. As I was getting into my pajamas she said, "Ray—I think we ought to go to church in the morning."

I looked at her. "What brought this on? This wouldn't have anything to do with our ghostly friend, would it?"

She got into her side of the bed and snuggled over to mine. "It might," she yawned. "But that's not important. Will you go? There's a special All Hallows service at Westminster Abbey tomorrow morning."

"We'll talk about it in the morning," I mumbled. With any luck she might oversleep and forget about it.

"Ray?"

"Hmmm?"

"Hold me tight."

I held her tight. But I couldn't make love to her. I suppose it was just another example of my overactive imagination but I had the feeling that we were being watched.

It was just after three by the luminous hands of the bedside clock when I awoke. The moon was down and the room was in darkness except for the eerie penumbra of all sleeping cities. I was turning over to go back to sleep when I heard it again. The dragging, shuffling noise. I sat up.

The noise stopped. I waited a few minutes and nothing happened. Then I heard what sounded like muffled voices. I got out of bed carefully and tiptoed to the door and opened it. The hall was amber from a distant streetlight. The whispering voices continued. They sounded just like Eddie and Richard talking in one of their rooms as they sometimes did when they thought we were asleep.

I crossed the hall and opened the door to Eddie's room and looked in. The bed was tidy. The room was empty. I closed the door and went to look in Richard's room. I don't know what I was expecting to find. The boys had no key and could not have gotten back into the house without our hearing them. Richard's room was empty, too. Yet there was that *feeling* that someone was there. In each room.

I closed the door and went back down the hall to our room. Still the whispering sound was there, indistinct, but there nevertheless. I went to the banister and peered into the downstairs hall. There was no sound there. I came back. The whispering was beginning to fade. It could have been a whisper of the wind. But there was no wind.

Somebody could be playing a distant radio. With all these old houses joined together the sound would carry in the still of the night. But it wasn't that kind of sound.

It suddenly dawned on me that the sound was coming from above my head. I looked up. The trapdoor.

The whispering stopped.

I waited, looking up at the trapdoor. It was at least ten feet from the floor to the ceiling. The only ladder in the house was the kitchen step stool and that wouldn't help. For the boys to get up there would be impossible. Anyway, what would make them want to play a stupid prank like that?

I turned away and went back to bed. Just as I closed my eyes I heard it again. Whispering and gurgling. Of course! That damned tank!

But as I burrowed back under the covers the uneasy thought came into my drowsy mind that the tank made an entirely different kind of noise from the one I had heard. Didn't it? I slipped over the edge of sleep and forgot about trying to answer.

"You've just got ten minutes to drink this cup of coffee, shave, and get dressed," Liz was saying briskly.

I opened a bleary eye. "What's the matter with you?" I groaned. "It's Sunday. Go back to bed!"

· "We're going to church, remember? All Hallows. Westminster Abbey."

I opened both eyes. She was serious. "You go pray for your ghost," I told her. "I'll stay here in case he comes looking for company. If he's as lonesome as you say it would be inhospitable to have him find his old haunt empty."

I thought that was a pretty good pun for somebody half-asleep, but Liz was adamant. She took her car keys from her purse and held them before my face. "I am going to get the car. You can have your coffee while you shave. I expect to find you fully dressed when I get back." She went out and shut the door in a no-nonsense sort of way.

There was nothing I could do about it. I swung both legs out of bed and lit a cigarette, staring gloomily out at the brilliant autumn sunlight. The first of November. Forty-four more shopping days till Christmas. I took a sip of coffee and stood up. Nicotine, caffeine, and blood began to mix and circulate. I stumbled toward the bathroom.

I have only a vague recollection of the ride to the Abbey, Liz driving. A vivid recollection of Liz giving me the elbow treatment to keep me from dozing through the service. In between she was busy doing something about her ghost, head bowed, looking sweet and angelic. I began to count the rows of scaffolding on a repair job in the corner just to keep awake. It was like counting sheep. Liz shook me. "You can wake up now—it's all over," she was saying, louder than she needed to. Several people had the poor manners to grin as I followed her out of the pew.

I drove home, wide awake. We stopped and bought some cigarettes and the Sunday papers. I let Liz out in front of the house and put the car away. When I got back there was a glorious smell of frying bacon as I opened the door. I sat at the breakfast table with a cup of coffee and read the papers while Liz broke four eggs into the pan. A story on the front page of the *Sunday Telegraph* caught my eye.

"Hey, Liz—you know all that scaffolding we saw in the Abbey this morning? Listen to this. It says that workmen doing repairs inside the Abbey discovered yesterday morning that the urn containing the bones of the princes murdered in the Tower is missing. Police suspect that it is some kind of student prank."

I put more bread in the toaster and read on: "The oones were originally found in 1674 during alterations at the Tower of London and at the command of Charles II were reburied in the Abbey. In 1933 the urn containing the bones was opened and an examination made by Professor William Wright, at that time the president of the Anatomical Society of Great Britain and Ireland. Professor Wright concluded that the bones were the remains of two brothers whose ages corresponded to those of the princes and that the skull of the eldest gave evidence of death by suffocation, thus strengthening the assumption that the bones were in fact those of the murdered princes. The remains were replaced and the urn resealed on July 11, 1933, and it had been in the Abbey ever since, until found missing yesterday."

"All very appetizing stuff just before breakfast," Liz said, bringing in the eggs.

We spent a lazy day doing nothing much, but I couldn't help feeling tense. About three o'clock we went out for a long walk in the crisp November air, down to St. James's Park where we fed the ducks. Where were Eddie and Richard at this moment, I wondered. Then, feeling hungry ourselves, we strolled back home for dinner. It was fully dark by five and we sat for several hours dozing with our feet up, papers scattered all over the place, the television talking to itself. The phone rang.

Liz went to answer. I could hear her talking in the hall, but I couldn't hear what she was saying because of the television. She came back looking worried.

"Anything wrong?" I asked.

"That was Nancy Marlwood. She phoned to invite us and the boys down there next weekend."

"You and the boys can go if you want to."

She shook her head absently as though concerned with something else. "I told her you had to start writing and we'd come another time." Her eyes went to the clock on the mantel. It said a quarter to nine. "Ray, don't you think it's time the boys were home?"

"What time did they leave down there?"

She hesitated. "Nancy didn't really know. They left early this morning to go look at a few old castles and things and she didn't really expect them back. They took a lunch with them. Nancy thought they would just drive on back to London when they finished sight-seeing—but she seemed a little surprised they weren't back yet."

"Well, they probably overdid it. You know how boys are. Anyway, they've got Sir James with them."

Liz stood looking at me for a full five seconds before I caught on.

"He's not with them. He left last night. Right after we did."

I stood up wondering what the hell to do. I didn't like this. Nor, this time, did Liz. I could see it in her face. She came over and put her arms around me. "Ray—now don't start thinking those things about Sybil and Bunting. It's not that that I'm worried about."

"Well what else is there to worry about, for God's sake?"

"They might have been in an accident."

I lit a cigarette and started to pace the floor. I stopped and looked at the clock. "Well give it an hour. If we don't hear anything by a quarter to ten I'm going to phone the police."

Liz nodded. There was something almost evasive in the way she did it. I had the feeling she was trying to hide something. I went over and put my finger under her chin, making her look at me. Her nose was twitching slightly.

"Liz. There's more, isn't there?"

She nodded again. And swallowed. "Last night, before we left, Nancy and I took the boys up to put them to bed, remember? Well, when we got up there they asked if they could have a look at the moon through Roger's telescope. I said, well, all right—so long as they didn't stay up too late. Then I came back downstairs and we went home."

"And they didn't go straight to bed."

"No, Nancy said . . ." Liz stopped, afraid to go on. Afraid of my reaction.

"Go on, Liz," I said, keeping my voice calm.

"Well, it was such a nice night. Moonlight and everything. Sybil suggested—that it might be fun . . ."

"If they all went for a midnight stroll in the moonlight," I finished for her.

"Yes," Liz said in a whisper.

"And of course Nancy and Roger said they'd stay and do the dishes while the others went for a walk."

"Yes."

I turned away.

"Ray—you can't really believe . . . !"

"Okay, I'm crazy! I've got a kink about this thing. What's wrong with a couple of people going for a moonlight stroll at midnight and taking two boys along? I'll tell you. Nothing. Under ordinary circumstances. But I'll tell you something else, Liz. If they get home safely tonight, if there is nothing more irregular to this than the fact that a couple of young boys were kept up past their bedtime— then I will pick up that phone in the morning and make that appointment as I promised. And believe me, the way

I feel right now it will be a cheap price to pay for peace of mind."

I stubbed out my cigarette and lit another. The television was making a terrible racket and I switched it off. The sudden quiet was unnerving. I put a Rachmaninoff on the hi-fi and let it thunder.

The phone rang again.

Liz and I nearly collided trying to answer it. I got there first.

"Hello?"

"Ah, Ray old chap—there you are! James Tyrell here."

"Sir James! Have you . . . ?"

"Hang on—somebody here wants to talk to you."

Liz was looking at me in an agony of suspense. I tilted the receiver so that she could hear.

"Dad?"

"Eddie?"

Liz's face broke into a smile of relief. "Where are they?" she whispered. Between Rachmaninoff pounding away in the front room and Liz hissing in one ear while Eddie shouted—he always mistrusted the phone to carry his voice of its own accord—into the other I didn't absorb everything at once, but I gathered they had a good day's castle hunting with Sybil and Bunting and near sundown they found they were close to Romsey in the New Forest, so they dropped in at The Shires to visit Sir James and he asked them to stay to dinner.

"When will you be home?" I asked.

"Sir James asked if we could stay overnight. That's why we phoned. Can we, Dad? Please? He's got some super old swords and armor and things he said we could look at."

Liz and I looked at each other uncertainly. Then Sir James came back on the line. "Are you there, Ray? Listen, I thought since these lads of yours were enjoying themselves so much it would be a shame to break it up. Besides, if they drove back now with Sybil and Father Bunting it would be deucedly late when they . . ."

"Oh—are Sybil and Bunting coming back tonight?" The relief in my voice must have been obvious.

"Yes, old chap. That's why I'm ringing you. I have to drive up to town in the morning anyway. I could drop your lads at your place in plenty of time to pick up their school books."

Liz was nodding. "Oh, well, in that case . . ." I said.

"Splendid! We'll see you in the morning then."

"Hang on a minute, Sir James—Liz wants a word with one of the boys."

Liz took the phone. "Eddie? Now you two behave yourselves, do you hear? And don't stay up too late like you did last night."

I leaned close to the earpiece to catch his reply.

"Heck, Mom, we weren't up late. We just went for a little walk, that's all. In the moonlight. It was fun. Anyway, who told you?"

"Never you mind. Just remember that I always find out when you do things you're not supposed to."

"Okay, Mom. We'll be good. See you tomorrow."

Liz hung up and looked at me. Then we both laughed and hugged each other. "Oh, Ray—thank God everything is all right."

I looked at my watch. "Look, I've got a great idea. We've got the house to ourselves. It's still early. How about a nice hot bath, a couple of drinks to set the mood, and then"—I pulled her close and kissed her—"we can make love in the living room in front of the fire."

We both overslept the following morning because I forgot to set the alarm clock. It was half-past eight when Liz tumbled out of bed. She had a nine o'clock appointment at Pinewood Studios. I could afford to be more leisurely. The search rooms at the Public Record Office wouldn't be open till nine thirty. I made coffee and toast, left hers on the kitchen table, and took mine upstairs while I shaved. The coffee was good but the toast and marmalade gummed up my electric razor and I was trying to clean it out when the doorbell rang.

A minute later I heard Sir James's voice booming heartily in the downstairs hall, followed by subdued monosyllables from Eddie and Richard and some worried dialogue from Liz in a querulous tone. I went to the head of the stairs and leaned over the banister.

"Good morning, Sir James," I called. "Thanks for delivering the boys." Then I caught sight of Liz's face. "Anything wrong?"

Sir James gave a deprecatory laugh and waved a bandaged hand. "Just a slight scratch, old chap. An accident. Nothing to worry about."

I went downstairs, Eddie and Richard watching me with hangdog looks. "What happened?" I asked Liz.

"Your sons were fooling around with dangerous weapons and nearly killed Sir James."

"Nonsense, my dear!" Tyrell laughed.

"Eddie?" I said, waiting for him to explain.

He looked pointedly at Richard who hung his head sheepishly. "It was my fault, Dad. We were on our way upstairs to bed and I saw this old halberd hanging there and . . . well, I leaned out over the banister to feel if it had a sharp edge and . . . it fell."

"My fault entirely, Ray," Sir James boomed. "Should have fastened the damn thing more securely. Could have happened anytime. Luckily I heard it crashing down and stepped back. Tip of it only grazed my hand."

I made profuse apologies while Liz, grim-faced, sent the boys to gather their school things. Sir James insisted on making light of it, but I felt upset about the incident and told him I'd see the boys got a good talking to.

After further apologies from us, and further deprecation from Sir James, he left, laughing as he waved his bandaged right hand and shook hands left-handed. When he had gone Liz turned to me. "And what did *you* promise to do this morning?"

"I haven't forgotten."

"A promise is a promise. Come on, you two, or you'll be late for school." She bustled them out the front door and I watched them follow her across the square toward the mews garage. I looked at my watch. If I stopped to phone for a doctor's appointment now I might not get a seat at the Public Record Office. I would phone at lunch time.

The morning paper, late again, was on the mat as I went out. I picked it up to read on the underground. I was still reading, and trying to turn the page in the morning crush at Tottenham Court Road, when my eye caught an item on the back page of the paper held by the man next to me.

VANDALS HOLD
BLACK MASS
IN COUNTRY CHURCH

Vandals broke into All Hallows Church, Elhamstead, Sussex, sometime after midnight on Saturday (Halloween, the Eve of the Feast of All Hallows). Four valuable sixteenth-century paintings depicting the Crucifixion were desecrated, among other damage. Stubs of four black candles found on the altar, plus certain other signs, indicate that a "Black Mass" may have been held.

Police believe that members of a Black Magic cult may have been responsible and are anxious to trace four persons, two adults and two children, who were seen in the vicinity just after midnight.

The damage was discovered when the verger came to open the church for Sunday morning services yesterday.

Suddenly, I felt sick. The train ground to a stop at Holborn and I shoved my way to the exit, not caring that it was the wrong stop. Claustrophobia assailed me. I had to escape from the press of people, up from the underground to the sane light of day where I could collect my thoughts. I found myself down Kingsway, bumping into hurrying office-goers, drawing strange glances. All Hallows Church, Elhamstead—the same words that had been written on the back of the snapshot of Bunting and Sybil that I had found in her handbag.

I stopped in Her Majesty's Stationery Office in Kingsway and bought an ordinance survey map of Sussex. My hands shook as I laid it open on the counter and searched the area around Battle. There it was. Elhamstead. Less than a mile from Marlwood's cottage. Where did I go from here?

Indecision is personal purgatory especially when it involves two children whom you love very much. I wandered on down Kingsway and cut across toward Chancery Lane and the Public Record Office. I stepped off the curb, heard a woman scream, the screech of brakes, then the voluble profanity of a Cockney taxi driver. I mumbled an apology and stepped back on the curb to await the green pedestrian light.

If I phoned Liz at Pinewood she might accuse me of the same old witch-hunt. Besides, if she agreed with me, there would be the agony of decision—to phone the police and say we suspected our own sons of being two of the Black Magic practitioners? Or could we shield them from the crude public mercy of the law by taking them to . . . to whom? Priest? Psychiatrist? Was it witchcraft? Was it evil? Or just another case of coincidence?

I stopped in a phone booth in Chancery Lane and dialed the area code and number for Pinewood Studios. Before the phone started to ring I hung up and walked out. Too many times before I had been certain, and each time there had been a perfectly logical explanation that proved me wrong.

I turned in past the gatekeeper at the Public Record Office and walked down the path. It was starting to rain, a chill November drizzle from a leaden sky which matched my spirits. Suddenly I stopped. There was no point in going inside. I could no more concentrate on research for my novel than play chess against a computer. I turned back to the street where I flagged a cab and asked the driver to take me to the British Museum.

In the vast domed hush of the Reading Room an hour later I was hunched over a stack of books on the reign of Richard III. Just why, I could not explain. There was a strange compulsion about it, engendered by recollections of things that did not fit. Or perhaps fitted too well. The coincidence in the names of the princes in the Tower being the same as those of my own sons, the disappearance of the urn from Westminister Abbey. Improbables? Perhaps. But—impossible?

When I first began to read I was seized with panic, then by main strength I forced myself into a state of almost hypnotic concentration until the words on the pages before me stood out in cold clarity, devoid of personal emotional involvement insofar as was humanly possible.

As I stood up to leave the Reading Room I glanced at the clock. I was astonished to find that it was nearly two in the afternoon. I had sat reading, entranced, for over four hours. As I gathered up my books one of the assistants came up, glanced at my seat number, then checked it with a note in his hand.

"Mr. Armacost?"

He handed me the slip of paper. "Inspector Talbot wants you to ring him at New Scotland Yard. Here's the number."

I put the books back down and walked, almost ran, to the phone in the corridor. It took an agonizing three minutes for them to locate the whereabouts of Inspector Talbot. "He isn't here, Mr. Armacost, but you can contact him at this number." I fumbled in my coat pocket for something to write on, found an old letter, jotted down the number. Then I realized it was my own.

Liz answered, her voice breaking over "hello."

"Liz! What's happened?"

"Oh, Ray, my God where have you *been?* I thought you said you'd be at the Public Record Office and ever since the police got in touch with me at Pinewood and told me he was dead I've been going crazy trying to . . ."

"Liz! *Who's* dead?"

"Him. The old man at the school. You know, the caretaker."

My feeling of relief that it was not one of the boys was immediately replaced by one of ominous dread. Miles Forest was dead. I had almost come to expect it. "Where are the boys?" I asked.

There was a moment of silence.

"Liz?"

"Ray. They haven't turned up at school. They've run away. Ray, come home, will you, for God's sake!"

"I'll take a taxi right away," I snapped and hung up.

As I darted for the exit I dropped the letter on which I had jotted the phone number. Automatically I picked it up. As I did so the name Tyrell caught my eye. It was the letter from the Sotheby's appraiser, the one I had never fully read. I read it now.

. . . the legend has it that Richard III gave it to Sir James Tyrell, presumably for his part in the murder of the princes, Richard and Edward, in the Tower. The legend further states that because of this there was a curse attached to the table. It disappeared from the Tyrell family sometime in the early- or mid-sixteenth century (see Osgood's *Legends of Old England*, p. 218).

I didn't wait to read any more. John Dighton had been the first to die. Now the caretaker, Miles Forest. That left Sir James Tyrell. And my research that afternoon had disclosed that all three were namesakes, and, in Sir James's case at least, direct descendants, of the three men responsible for the murder of the princes in the Tower. I turned back to the phone, dug my wallet from my pocket, found Sir James's card, and dialed his number at King's Southerton.

His housekeeper answered. No, Sir James was not at home. He had phoned from London with a message for his gamekeeper to say that he would return home later that afternoon.

"Then where can I find him?" I almost yelled at her.

There was indignation in her voice when she replied,

"I'm sure I don't know, sir, but you might try his London flat." She gave me the number. I rang off without even the courtesy of saying good-bye and dialed his London number. It rang for a full two minutes. No answer. I ran outside into the November rain and jumped into a taxi.

There was a police Volvo with a uniformed constable behind the wheel standing at the curb when the taxi dropped me in front of the house. I ran up the steps just as the door was opened by a plainclothes detective.

I ran into the living room. Liz jumped up when she saw me and I held her close.

She was trying hard to keep her emotions under control but I could tell that she was near the breaking point. I turned to the Inspector, a crisp, efficient-looking man of about thirty-five.

"Can you tell me what's happened?"

"There seems to have been an accident at the school. The caretaker was firing the boiler this morning when he must have suffered a heart attack. He fell forward—into the boiler."

I winced. "God, what a way to die."

"Yes, it was rather ghastly."

"But—if it's an accident, why are you here, Inspector?"

He looked a bit embarrassed. "It is a trifle unorthodox to involve the Yard in something like this, but—well, to be quite blunt, Mr. Armacost, there was a previous incident, a prank I believe, involving your two lads. It seems that the headmaster thinks they may have had something to do with this morning's business. He insisted it be handled by Scotland Yard rather than the local police. And since the sons of some quite influential persons attend his school, some—er, strings were pulled, I believe. I thought, since we were already here, that we might as well get a description of your boys and pass it along to the Metropolitan Police."

I walked to the window and looked out. I could feel Liz's eyes on my back. When I turned around she was staring at me imploringly. But she had no reason to worry. Whatever lay behind this macabre sequence of events, I had a deep-rooted conviction that our sons were not really to blame. Involved, perhaps. But not of their own volition. They were only the instruments, not the perpetrators. Until such time as there was firm legal evidence that they had done something wrong my duty as a father was to try to protect them. And to extricate them from whatever evil force held sway over them.

For just a moment I thought of telling Talbot of my suspicions concerning Sybil and Bunting. One look at his face changed my mind. How do you tell a clear-minded, logical, scientifically trained detective inspector that you believe your sons are under the influence of witchcraft?

"Inspector, are our boys being accused of anything?"

"On present evidence, no."

"What does that mean?"

"Simply that we feel they may be able to help us with our inquiries."

The stock answer of the British police.

"Yet they are under suspicion because they are missing?"

"Not really. I should imagine that as soon as they heard what had happened to the caretaker they ran. Thinking, in view of their previous prank, that they might be blamed for this. We made a thorough investigation of the scene of the accident, Mr. Armacost. It was apparently well known that Miles Forest had a bad heart. I should say he became ill, possibly had a heart attack while stoking the boiler, stumbled, and fell forward into the flames."

"Could an autopsy show the cause of death?"

Talbot frowned. "It might be difficult. There were only the legs left."

Liz gave an involuntary gasp of horror.

"Our primary purpose in trying to trace the boys is simply a matter of their own safety," Talbot went on. "I don't relish the idea of two young lads abroad in London at night. There are some ugly people about. If you could give us any idea of where they might have gone . . . any friends, neighbors, relatives . . . ?"

I thought quickly. This could be a way to protect Sir James and at the same time deter the boys without arousing undue suspicion.

"We have a friend near Romsey in the New Forest. A Sir James Tyrell. They could have gone there."

"Oh, Ray . . . surely!" Liz said in astonishment.

But Talbot already had his notebook out. I gave him the address and phone number at King's Southerton. "Right, we'll alert the Romsey police and get them to send a car around." He put away his notebook and beckoned to Sergeant Digby. "Thank you for your help, Mr. Armacost. We'll keep you informed of any developments."

When they had gone Liz threw her arms around me. "Oh, thank God, Ray! I thought for a moment there you were going to tell him . . ."

I prised her arms gently away. "Liz—sit down. *Please*."

Her eyes met mine with that strange look I was beginning to know so well. A look of pity because of my strange behavior.

"Liz, tell me your maiden name."

Her look of pity intensified, but she played along with the air of someone humoring a lunatic. "Elizabeth Woodville," she recited like a schoolgirl.

"Right. Now, Liz, I want you to listen carefully, and stop looking at me that way. I spent several hours today doing research at the Reading Room. And what I found out has given me some possible explanation of just what the hell's going on. Promise you'll bear with me."

She nodded.

"Promise."

"All right, Ray—I promise." It was a hoarse whisper.

"The wife of King Edward the Fourth of England was named Elizabeth Woodville."

I waited for some reaction. She just looked at me. "It's—a common enough English name. After all, my ancestors came from this country."

"Yes, but do you know *when?*"

"Sometime after the Mayflower. My grandmother had an old Bible with some dates in it. I'm not quite sure."

"In 1648," I said firmly. "And Jeremiah Woodville, your direct ancestor, was also a direct descendant from the family of the Elizabeth Woodville who was the wife of Edward the Fourth."

"I—I didn't know that."

"And she had two sons, Richard and Edward, who, when they were aged twelve and ten—the same ages as our boys—were murdered. The princes in the Tower."

She swallowed uneasily. "Ray—aren't you reading a lot into coincidence again?"

"Let me finish!" She sat uneasily on the edge of her chair and glanced around, as though looking for a way to escape. "According to tradition," I went on, "the princes were murdered in the Tower in 1483, probably in August, nobody is quite certain. Nobody, that is, except our two sons who gave the date during a school history test as the *twenty-third* of August."

"Well?" Liz said.

"They gave the same date *independently*, in different rooms, at different times. They *knew* the right date, don't you *see?*

"Ray—what are you trying to say?" There was a touch of fear in her voice now.

"I think you know. But let me tell you the rest, and then you can make up your own mind whether or not I'm just a crank with a writer's imagination. When the princes were murdered their assassins were two men named . . . John Dighton and Miles Forest."

Liz caught her breath. The look of pity for me was gone now and in its place was a plea for denial—in the dawning realization that perhaps I might be right after all. "Oh, Ray—my *God!*"

"And there's more. Here, look." I took Sotheby's letter out of my pocket and showed her the paragraph about the origin of the Florentine table. She sat in disbelief as I folded the letter away. "And something else I found out this afternoon. This house we're in right now stands on the site of an inn called the Red Dragon where, on that August night in 1483, the original Sir James Tyrell met with Miles Forest and John Dighton to plot the murder of the princes in the Tower."

Liz was staring at me in horror. "That leaves only one namesake still alive," she whispered.

I nodded. "And last night James Tyrell just missed being killed when a halberd dropped on him from an up-stairs landing."

Liz dropped her face in her hands and began to sob.

"God, Ray, *no!* Our boys . . . my babies! They couldn't . . . *kill* anyone."

I knelt and took her in my arms. This time she did not draw away. "No, sweetheart, of course they couldn't," I soothed. *"They* couldn't kill anyone. Not of their own volition. But supposing some force has taken them over—some catalyst between good and evil . . ." There was just a flicker of that old look in her eyes but it was only a shadow and it was gone in an instant as I went on. "If they are not the"—I found it difficult to say the words—"the reincarnation of the princes, then at least these two evil persons, one posing as a Jesuit priest, the other undoubtedly a witch, have exploited this coincidence of names and have brainwashed these boys into believing, perhaps under the influence of drugs from one of those weird plants, that they *are* the reincarnation and must avenge their murders of five centuries ago."

She stared at me. "I—my brain has gone numb, Ray. I just find it impossible to believe. Sybil and Bunting?"

I stood up. "Did I tell you what went through my mind as I was coming home in the taxi a while ago? About their names?" She shook her head. "Take Bunting, for a start. Did you know that 'bunting' was a term of endearment for a witch's 'familiar'?

"And the name Sybil," I went on, "is another word for witch. And do you know why she spells her last name R-o-d-n-e, without a 'y'? Spell it backwards and see what you get."

Liz bit her lip in concentration. "E-n-d-o-r, Endor."

"Right—and the biblical witch of Endor, the sorceress nonpareil, led Saul to his death by hypnotic suggestion—or something a hell of a lot like it—on the eve of the battle of Gilboa. How's that for coincidence?"

"And if you spell 'noon' backwards it still comes out 'noon.' How's *that* for coincidence?" She lowered her head wearily into her hands. "Oh, Ray—what can we do?"

I poured us each a stiff Scotch. She took hers and looked at me imploringly. "I don't know," I said. "As soon as the police find the boys we'll see that they get some kind of treatment. Psychiatric, medical. Maybe even exorcism." I downed my drink in a gulp. "But first of all I'm going next door to have a word with Sybil."

Liz stood up. "I'm coming with you. But be careful, Ray. You've got no real proof. What are you going to do?"

I put my glass on the table. "I'm going to choke the truth out of her. Come along and watch."

I started for the door.

9

W<small>E</small> <small>WENT DOWN OUR FRONT STEPS QUICKLY, WITHOUT</small> coats, and shivered on Sybil's doorstep while I rang the bell. Nobody came.

"Have you seen her today?" I asked.

"I came over here when I heard the boys were missing. I thought they might have run to her. But she was out."

A sudden panic seized me when she said that. Supposing Sybil and Bunting had taken the boys? I stepped back and raised my foot.

"What are you doing?"

"I'm going to kick the goddamn door down and see what's going on!"

Just then the door opened and a woman stood there. Not Sybil, but a very attractive younger woman, well dressed in a casual but expensive-looking sort of way. I lowered my foot.

"Er—is Mrs. Rodne in?"

She looked puzzled. "Mrs. who?"

"Rodne," Liz said. "Syoil Rodne."

The woman shook her head. "I'm afraid I've never heard of her."

I was staring past her into the hall when a funny feeling began creeping over me, like a million cockroaches skittering over my skin. Gone were the plum-colored wallpaper and chocolate draperies and dark paint and gloomy Victoriana. The hall was bright with modern decor; cerise carpeting wall to wall and up the white-painted staircase. A small wrought-iron table, glass topped, held a stainless-steel sculpture. Framed splotches of color on the walls showed a preference for abstract art.

Liz had seen it too and was staring open-mouthed. We exchanged glances, then I turned to the woman who was now looking a bit annoyed. "Forgive us—we're the Armacosts from next door and we . . ."

Her expression brightened, welcoming. "Oh, the American writers! Yes, we'd heard you'd moved in. Forgive me for keeping you standing there in the cold—do come in."

We followed her into the welcome warmth of the hall as she chattered, leading us toward the living room. A youngish man, prematurely gray, laid aside a book and stood up when we entered.

"My husband," the young woman said. "We're Ted and Eunice Scotney. Darling, these are the Americans from next door. Mr. and Mrs . . . ?"

"Armacost," I said. "Liz and Ray."

The man shook hands and asked us to sit. "Would you care for a drink?"

Liz and I were looking around the room, brightly lit, furnishings as modern as tomorrow. We looked again at each other in disbelief.

Scotney noticed and gave a little laugh. "Is something wrong?"

"When—when did you move in?" I stammered.

"Well, we got back from abroad only yesterday morning. But we've lived here—at least we've had the house—for four years."

"You've been . . . *away?*" Liz managed to ask.

"In Singapore," Eunice said. "Ted is in the diplomatic service."

"So you rent the house while you're away?" I looked around. "You've certainly managed a transformation in a short time. When Sybil was here the place . . ."

It was their turn to exchange puzzled glances. "Transformation? You've been in here before?"

"Why—yes. We were friendly with your tenant, Mrs. Rodne. As a matter of fact—could you tell us where she's gone? It's important that we find her."

"This house has been closed for eighteen months," Scotney said. "We did let it once, but it was an unfortunate experience—so the last time we were home on leave we decided it was better to leave it empty. Do you mean to say someone has been *living* here?"

I looked at Liz. She was very pale. "Oh, God, Ray."

"What did you mean by 'transformation'?" Eunice Scotney asked.

I swallowed. "You'll have to excuse us," I said. "We were . . . *acquainted* with the woman living here. We thought it was her house. We didn't know . . ."

Liz asked in astonishment, "But what did she do with all the old Victorian furniture, all the old pictures? And the paint and wallpaper? She couldn't have changed all *that* in one night."

"But—the house is exactly as we left it!" Eunice said.

Liz was holding my hand now, trembling. "Ray—hadn't we better tell the police?"

"Would you mind telling us just what the devil is going on here? Police?"

"Look, Mr. Scotney—something most—unusual has happened. I'm not quite sure what, but it isn't good. I've had my suspicions about Mrs. Rodne and I've already been in touch with the police. Now our two young boys are missing from school and I'm afraid—afraid something may have happened to them. If you'll excuse us, please—I'll try to explain later. If I can. But before we go, could I ask a favor? I'd like to take a look at your back garden."

"Back garden?" Scotney said. "There's only the swimming pool."

He led us toward the back, past a superbly modern kitchen, all tile and stainless steel. From inside the back door he switched on the floodlights and we stood looking out on a swimming pool, empty now save for a few autumn leaves swirling in the corners. The only plants were evergreens in tubs.

We made hasty apologies for the intrusion, promising again to explain as best we could later, and left. No wonder Sybil had said that we were the only neighbors who had spoken to her since she lived there!

As we came into our own hall, the telephone was ringing. I snatched it up, Liz crowding close to listen.

"Ray, old chap? Tyrell here. You left a message for me to phone."

"Sir James? Thank God. Now I want you to listen carefully—this is urgent. There's been an accident at the boys' school and . . ."

He broke in reassuringly. "Yes, yes—I know all about it and everything is all right. Your lads are here with me now."

Liz and I looked at each other. "With *you?*" I asked.

"Yes. You see, after the last prank—oh, they told me all about it—they rather imagined they might be blamed for what happened this time. So I suppose they knew I had an understanding nature and would sort of take them in until I could reach you and explain that they had nothing to do with it. They hitchhiked here—would you believe it?! Saucy little devils. Anyway, don't worry. They can stay here the night and I'll drive them up the first thing in the morning."

"No!" I almost shouted. "Sir James, you've got to listen to me. Sybil Rodne has disappeared. Under circumstances that are, to say the least, peculiar."

"Really? Well, can't say I'm too surprised—she's an odd lot, that one."

"I think she's a witch."

He laughed. "Bitch? I say, that's a trifle harsh, isn't it? She's a queer old stick, but . . ."

"Witch, not bitch—*witch.* I believe she has the boys under some sort of hypnosis, either by drugs or some other way. I think they may have"—I swallowed hard, then forced myself to say it—"killed the old caretaker."

Liz turned away and started to cry.

"I say, you're not serious?"

"Very serious. I'll explain when I see you. Now please listen. I want you to lock yourself in your study. Don't let the boys near you until we or the police get there, under-

(180)

stand? Make some sort of excuse to your housekeeper and have somebody keep them occupied—*anybody*, but not you."

"But—why should they want to harm me?"

"I haven't the time to go into that now. Just do as I say. I'm going to phone the police right now. Then Liz and I will drive down."

"Very well, just as you say. Anyway, the boys are playing around in the barn at the moment. Seem to be having a whale of a time, judging from the row that's going on. You know what boys are."

I hung up feeling that I hadn't quite gotten the message across. Then I phoned Talbot at New Scotland Yard.

"I've found my sons. They are at Sir James Tyrell's." I told him my suspicions concerning Sybil and Bunting. "I want them picked up."

He hesitated. "On what specific charge, Mr. Armacost?"

"Hell, I don't know. Seduction of minor persons, corruption of morals, enticement—*any* goddamn thing."

"Serious charges, sir. Can you make them stick?"

"You're damn right I can."

"Very well, Mr. Armacost."

"And make sure the Romsey police get over to Tyrell's place right away."

"I've already told them your boys might be there. They've gone to investigate."

Liz was standing beside the Florentine table, pale and shaking, looking at it. "Have we got Nancy Marlwood's number?" I asked her.

"It's there on the phone pad." She stood watching me as I dialed, a zombielike expression on her face. She was in a state of shock. I reached out and took her hand. It was trembling. "Everything *will* be all right, won't it, Ray?"

I tried to smile reassuringly but my face felt like plaster. Nancy Marlwood answered.

"Nancy—this is Ray Armacost . . ."

"What a lovely surprise! How are you?"

"Not very well. Something's happened. Do you know where I can find Sybil?"

"Sybil?" There was a sudden change in her voice. A defensive note. "Why—no."

"Nancy, how much do you know about your sister's activities?"

There was a pause. "Well, to begin with, she's not really my sister. No relation, actually. We met at the garden club in the village some months back when she came to give a talk . . ."

I was holding the receiver so that Liz could hear.

". . . and we looked rather alike so this 'sister' thing grew up as something of a joke. Can you tell me what's happened?"

"I'm not really sure. Listen, Nancy—the other night at your place there was some mention of black magic. Do you know if Sybil and Father Bunting ever took a *serious* interest in it?"

Again there was a pause. Then Nancy said uneasily, "They did *talk* about it quite a lot at one stage. Roger got interested for a while—as he does with anything new. Then he . . ." She stopped.

"He what, Nancy?"

"Well—he got a bit frightened. Ray, I don't like to say anything against Sybil and Bunting—but, well, I did find them a bit—strange sometimes."

"Sure, I understand. Now just tell me this—did Sybil

ever give you an address where she could be found? Do you know where I might be able to find her now?"

"No, not really. She and Bunting just sort of came and went. Thought it was rather peculiar that she never wrote or invited us to her place. Maybe you could locate Bunting through the Jesuit headquarters."

I said good-bye and hung up. From my briefcase I took the notebook on which I had jotted the phone number I had overheard Bunting give to Sybil that day in the garden. I held it in my hand and dialed the number.

"Brompton Cemetery," a voice answered.

"Sorry," I said. "I must have misdialed. I was trying to get 352-1201."

"This *is* 352-1201," the man said.

I hung up. Funny, I could distinctly remember Sybil saying to Bunting, "What if anyone wanted to contact you by telephone?" And him chuckling as he answered, "They could always reach me at 352-1201." What was it Sybil had said then? Yes—"How very droll!" Droll? Macabre was more like it. Still, I had probably written the wrong number.

I thumbed through the directory for the Jesuit headquarters. When I dialed, a voice answered, "Society of Jesus, Father Charles speaking."

"Father Charles, my name is Ray Armacost. I'm trying to locate a friend of mine named Father George Bunting."

"Bunting?" The voice sounded a little dubious. I heard the rustle of pages as he checked the register. Then, "I don't recognize the name, Mr. Armacost. Are you certain Father Bunting is a Jesuit?"

"Well—no, I'm not."

"You might try the Carmelites out in Kensington. But I

haven't heard of a Jesuit named Bunting since the scandal of 1483."

My ears pricked up.

He chuckled. "Private joke. There was a notorious Father Bunting who went off the rails in 1483. Began dabbling in the occult—diabolism, that sort of thing. He was unfrocked and finally committed suicide. But I hardly think that's the Father Bunting you're looking for." He laughed.

"Father Charles—where was this unfrocked priest buried, do you know?"

"As a matter of fact, I do. In those days it was common practice to bury suicides in unconsecrated ground. There was a plot for suicide burials in what is now Brompton Cemetery."

"I see. Thank you, Father." I hung up and stood for a moment looking at the faces on the table. Surprisingly, they were cherubic.

Liz came down the stairs wearing her coat and pulling on her gloves. She looked tense, drawn. "Did you find him?" she asked.

I saw no point in burdening her with another gruesome detail. "Bunting? He's not available at the moment." I went upstairs to get my coat.

I glanced at my watch as I left the bedroom. It was half past four and nearly fully dark. I switched off the bedroom light and started for the stairs just as I heard Liz's terrified scream. From the landing I could see her cowering beside the front door, staring at the table, and screaming in continuous hysterical waves. I bounded down the stairs and caught her to me, turning her around so that she wouldn't see the table. She stopped screaming and began sobbing, "For God's sake, Ray, let's get out of here!" I turned to look at the table.

The faces were not only demoniacal, *they were moving*. Like a television picture with the sound turned down, they writhed and rolled their heads, leering, laughing obscenely, soundlessly. This was no optical illusion.

I opened the door and let her go out first. Before I followed I took one last look at the table. The faces were still moving, contorted with soundless laughter. I closed the door and led Liz across the square and around the mews to the garage. The faces had me in a growing panic. Each time before the gargoyles had portended some disaster. The night Dighton had come to the house. And when Dighton had died. And when Sir James had first seen them they had leered as though at a potential victim—but only he had seen them. Could their antics now be a portent of some dreadful *grand finale?*

As we drove out of the square Liz looked up at the house. "It was such a nice house. I was so sure we could be happy there. We *were* happy, Ray—until . . ." She didn't finish, but began to cry quietly. I didn't try to stop her.

We fell silent for a long time, as though we were both numbed by our inability to comprehend what was completely incomprehensible. It wasn't until we were swinging onto the M3 highway headed west that Liz turned to me again. "They will be all right, won't they, Ray? I mean, if Sybil has been drugging them or whatever, they can be cured, can't they?"

"Sure," I said. "Of course they can." I wanted to stop the car and cry my heart out, but I couldn't let her know I was afraid it was already too late.

"Or do you think it was something else—something really *evil*? Bunting wasn't really a priest, was he?"

"He—probably had been at one time."

"Then this—influence, or whatever it is, can be exorcised. Ray—let's go back home. Back to the States. You've got enough material for a couple of books by now. You could write them there.

"We'll go back," I said. "Just as soon as we can pack."

That seemed to satisfy her. "God, I feel tired. This day has been a hundred years long. All I want now is to see my babies."

I looked at her. She really meant it. A mother's love is a mysterious thing. She still really didn't believe this was happening. Her babies. I wondered if we would ever see them again.

For one thing, at least, I was thankful. Inspector Talbot had said he would alert the Romsey police. Sir James Tyrell was safe by now from the retribution of history. I wondered, vaguely, why fate had decreed that he should be spared and Forest and Dighton should not. Then I remembered the story I had read in the *Southwind* papers—the story of his ancestor who had been lashed to the wheel of his ship and murdered. The legend of the table's curse. Perhaps that had been satisfaction enough for whatever power of darkness had engineered this macabre vendetta. Perhaps.

We reached Romsey in an hour and a half and turned off the main highway onto the country road leading to the village of King's Southerton. As we neared the wooded hill behind the little Norman church where The Shires stood overlooking the valley I could see lights through the trees. I felt a sense of relief.

"We'll be there in a minute."

How would I act, I wondered, when I faced the boys, now knowing what I did? How could I go through life watching my sons grow to manhood, wondering when this fated thing would draw them back to this side of the world? For come back they would, I was certain of that. From what Talbot had said there would be no prosecution. From the official viewpoint the boys had not yet committed a crime. I could not help being glad about that.

Perhaps I should just let fate take its own course. What else could I do? Nobody believed me, with the possible exception of Liz who had been stunned by the transformation of Sybil's house and the sight of the writhing gargoyles. And even she, if I knew Liz, would eventually make some rationalization for what we had seen—perhaps by convincing herself that we had been drugged, or under the influence of hypnosis. And I? If I went around telling people that my sons were the second incarnation of the princes who had been slain in the Tower on the orders of their uncle Richard III I would soon be shut up in a laughing academy. No, the best thing I could do would be to keep quiet and watch carefully—for the rest of my life.

As I swung the car around the circular drive before the big half-timbered Tudor manor house the headlights picked out two police cars down by the barn. And another vehicle that looked like an ambulance. Liz saw them too. I stopped the car. We both ran toward the ambulance.

A small crowd of police stood around the barn. Two men were carrying an empty stretcher toward the barn door and just inside I caught the intense blue flash of photography. A uniformed constable blocked our path.

"Sorry, sir—you can't go in there."

"I'm Ray Armacost. This is my wife. We're looking for our little boys."

He gave us both a pitying look. "I'll tell the superintendent you're here."

We waited while he went over to a group of plainclothesmen standing just inside the barn door and spoke to one of them who began walking toward us.

"I'm Superintendent Devereaux. Your sons weren't here when we arrived. I was hoping you might have had some word."

He looked at Liz, then back at me. "Did you know Sir James Tyrell?"

"We both did." The past tense came automatically. Liz caught her breath.

"I'm afraid we need positive identification of two bodies. The housekeeper is hysterical and won't come out. There are no other servants on the premises. The gamekeeper's gone for the evening and we haven't been able to find him. Perhaps if you could assist us."

"I'll try," I said, with a horrible, hollow feeling in my chest. I started to follow him, then stopped in my tracks. "Superintendent—did you say *bodies?*"

"Yes, sir. A man and a woman. We think the man must be Sir James Tyrell, but we can't be certain. The other one—the lady—is unknown."

The police stepped back deferentially to let the superintendent through and I followed. An old farm wagon stood in the barn, a huge-wheeled, swayback haywain handcrafted from solid oak and at least a hundred and fifty years old. I couldn't see very well at first because the police photographer was blocking my view. His flash exploded and he turned away. Then I saw. They were each lashed to one of the big wheels. Spread-eagled. Stark naked and horribly mutilated.

I turned my head and vomited into a pile of straw in the corner.

"Sorry, sir," the superintendent said gently, coming up beside me. "I should have warned you—it's not a pretty sight. Are you all right?"

I wiped my mouth on a handkerchief, feeling dizzy. I nodded. "Yes—I'm all right."

"Do you know either of them?"

I turned and forced myself to look again. The smell of blood was sickening. Sybil's head was hanging by a single tendon, lolling across her great fat bloodstained breasts. Bunting's head was in two parts, but still recognizable. It had been split from top to chin. There were great gaping wounds in both their bodies. A bloodstained halberd lay on the stone floor beside the wagon. I turned away and quickly pushed through the police at the door into the welcome cold November air. I leaned against the wheel of a tractor, my empty stomach heaving violently. I wiped the sweat from my face as Devereaux came up with Liz.

"I'm sorry to press you, Mr. Armacost, but I must know. Can you make a positive identification?"

I nodded. "At least—I know who they're supposed to be."

The superintendent looked puzzled. "I don't quite understand."

"I'm not sure that I do either, superintendent."

Liz was beside herself. "Ray, who *are* they?"

"Sybil and Bunting," I told her.

Her reaction was instinctive. I should have been prepared for it. She gasped and turned to look toward the barn. In that instant a flashbulb lit the scene and she had an unobstructed view before someone closed the door. I caught her as she fainted.

When Liz regained consciousness I walked over to Devereaux and told him what I knew about Sybil Rodne and Father George Bunting. Or as much as I thought he would believe.

"Thank you, Mr. Armacost. I'll notify the Jesuit superior about Father Bunting."

And good luck, I thought.

"Oh, I shouldn't worry about the boys if I were you. If you say they were here with Sir James when you telephoned from London, then he has probably taken them someplace since he isn't here either."

"Not here!" I was puzzled. "What did the housekeeper say?"

"She was busy getting dinner and she didn't really pay much attention to what Sir James told her. She thinks he may have taken them to a cinema in Winchester or Southampton."

"You must find them as soon as you can. Can you send a car to look for them?"

"I'm afraid I don't see the urgency, Mr. Armacost. Our job is now to find whoever murdered these two people."

"That's what I mean. Don't say anything to my wife, but please, you must find them. Sir James and the boys may have seen something. They may not be safe either." I had to convince Devereaux to find the boys and Sir James but I couldn't bring myself to tell him the real reason for my fears.

Just than a constable came up and spoke to Devereaux. "Excuse me, sir, we've just located Sir James Tyrell. He's dead, sir."

Devereaux glanced at me, probably wondering where

the children might be if, in fact, they had not left the house with Tyrell.

"I don't think it's murder, sir. We found him in the library. We had to break down the door. He was just sitting there with a book in his lap. Apparently died of a heart attack."

Poor old boy, I thought. Well, he was better off than the rest of us who had gotten involved in this mess. At least his death had the blessing of normalcy. I pondered for a moment, trying to assess his part in this grisly charade. After all, Captain Sir James Tyrell of the *Southwind* had expiated his sins spread-eagled on the wheel of his ship. What fitting irony that Sybil and Bunting should die a similar death in his descendant's barn.

I glanced uneasily toward the barn. How exactly had Sybil and Bunting met their ghastly end? Strange that they should be spread-eagled on the wheels also. Who or what was responsible? They had, as far as I knew, no ancestors involved in the murder of the princes. Were they, as I had already surmised, merely the pawns of whatever force of evil was behind it? Themselves destroyed by that same force when their task was completed? For that matter, were they real at all? I thought of the original Father Bunting five centuries dead by his own hand in Brompton Cemetery. And the house in Bentley Square where Sybil had never lived. I shivered and turned away. Forget it, Armacost. All you want now is to get your boys back alive and well and to hell with everything else.

A terrifying thought suddenly struck me and I felt my knees go weak. What if my boys *had* been a reincarnation? And what now—now that vengeance on the descendants of their murderers had been wreaked to the full? Where would they go? Would they return, perfectly normal and healthy, as our sons, Richard and Eddie? Or would they simply retreat into the dusty pages of history whence they had come? No. Oh, my God—*no!* That just couldn't happen. Flesh and blood just didn't disappear. No, they were *real*. Our kids. I had seen them born, I had . . .

"Mr. Armacost?" Devereaux's voice seemed to come from far away. "I think we'd better search for the children."

I didn't hear him right away—my mind had gone back a year in time and three thousand miles to a lake in upper New York State. Liz and I and two young boys in a canoe, sunlight sparkling on water. Laughter. Other scenes flashed by; toboggans on crisp snow, more boyish laughter, starlight through tall pines—"Daddy, what makes a star twinkle?"

"Mr. Armacost?" I turned my head to look at him. "Do you have any idea at all where the boys might have gone?"

I shook my head. "They don't know a soul around here."

"I think you know something you're not telling me, Mr. Armacost," he said as gently as he could.

There was no point in telling him. What purpose would it serve now? Besides, it wouldn't change a goddamn thing. I shook my head. "I'm just worried about my wife. She's had about as much as she can take."

"Why doesn't she lie down for a while inside?" Devereaux suggested, indicating the house. "I'm sure the old housekeeper will be glad for the company. I'll send the police surgeon to give Mrs. Armacost a sedative." He turned to go, then stopped. "There is just one more thing."

"Yes?"

"Do you have anything personal belonging to your sons—an item of clothing, anything like that? I'm afraid I'll have to bring in tracker dogs to search the forest."

"There's an old sweater in the car, I think. As soon as I've got my wife to bed I'll get it."

"That'll do nicely." He started to walk away.

"Superintendent?"

"Don't tell my wife about the dogs."

"I understand."

I walked over to where Liz was sitting on the back step of the ambulance drinking a cup of tea brought by the driver.

"It'll be all right, Liz," I said automatically. They were empty words. She said nothing, just sipped her tea and stared straight ahead.

The police surgeon came up and introduced himself. Calm and reassuring, he gave Liz an injection. They put her on a stretcher and took her into the house. The housekeeper was pleased to have something to distract her attention, you could tell that. She fussed over Liz and put her to bed in one of the guest rooms—in a big four-poster with an electric blanket.

"I'll make you a nice hot drink, m'dear," she said, smiling at Liz, tucking her in.

I followed the woman into the hall and closed the door. For someone who had been in a state of hysterics she had made a good recovery. "Excuse me, Mrs . . . ?"

"Tranter, Elsie Tranter."

"Mrs. Tranter, could you tell me what happened? Or don't you feel up to it?"

"Oh, I'm all right now," she said in her Hampshire brogue. "But I fair went to pieces when I found they two there in the barn. I've seen a few things in my day, but . . ."

I nodded. "I know what you mean, Mrs. Tranter. But can you tell me when you last saw my boys?"

She knitted her brows. "I don't rightly know, sir. They

was playing in the barn lot when I was preparin' dinner. I do remember Sir James comin' to tell me somethin', but I didn't pay much attention—I was that busy. I realized now he said something about he would be in his study if he was wanted. Then I found I hadn't no eggs in the larder for the Yorkshire pudding and I went down to the hen run to get some. When I passed the barn the light was on and the door was open and I looked in and saw . . ." She broke off and closed her eyes, shaking her head quickly as if to drive away the memory.

"Where were the boys?"

She opened her eyes. "I don't know. I haven't seen them since."

"When did Bunting and Sybil Rodne arrive?"

Again she shook her head. "I've no idea. First time I knew they was around was when I found—that mess in the barn. Well, now—I'll make your wife a nice hot cup of Ovaltine. It'll help her sleep."

She bustled off toward the downstairs kitchen and I went back into the bedroom to find Liz was already asleep. I was glad. I needed time to think. I kissed her cheek and went down to the kitchen and told Mrs. Tranter to forget the Ovaltine.

I went back outside just as two police vans pulled into the barn lot. "The dog-handlers have just arrived," Devereaux said. "If you wouldn't mind getting that sweater."

It was on the back window shelf. Eddie's. I felt funny carrying it over to Devereaux. As I handed it to him I noticed the Snoopy badge Eddie had sewn on the front. It read, "I love mankind—it's people I can't stand." I felt the tears start again. Devereaux noticed and took the sweater without saying a word.

I walked with him to where the two uniformed constables were taking their Alsatians from the vans. Devereaux handed over the sweater. "One of the boys' sweaters, constable. I don't think you'll have much trouble. Chances are they saw what was happening here, got scared, and ran to hide in the forest."

From the way the two constables looked at him I knew they didn't believe him. They glanced at me and looked away.

"Here, Prince," one of them said, holding the sweater toward his dog.

An ironic touch—that the dog should be named Prince.

The Alsatian whimpered and drew away from the proffered sweater. The constable, with his superintendent looking on, grew annoyed. He tried to calm the dog, but the animal only cowered and pulled away, trying to slip the leash over its head, whimpering and struggling.

"How long have you been handling dogs, constable?" Devereaux asked sarcastically.

"Long enough, sir!" He handed the sweater to his companion. "Here, Jock—you have a go while I get Prince settled down." He led his dog away, talking to it quietly. Once beyond our vicinity the dog recovered, tail wagging, tongue lolling merrily as he turned and looked back.

The second dog reacted in identical fashion. After a short struggle, Jock too admitted defeat, red-faced. "I don't know what's wrong with him tonight, sir!" he told Devereaux. "I've only seen him act this way once before and that was in a house that was supposed to be haunted."

"Well, there are no ghosts around here, constable!" Devereaux said sharply. "Exercise your dogs for a minute and then come back and try again."

I turned away. I felt old and extremely tired. I lit a cigarette and walked across the lawn to the walled garden at the rear of the house. I stood looking up at the light in the window of the bedroom where Liz lay sleeping. She could not remain under sedation forever. Tomorrow, the next day—*sometime* she would have to be told about what happened today. Just what, I wasn't quite sure myself. But whatever it might be, it would not be easy to live with. For either of us.

Devereaux found me there a few minutes later. "There's been a phone call for you. An Inspector Talbot wants you to ring him at your home."

I felt a tingle of alarm.

"Did he tell you why?"

I could tell Devereaux was hedging. "It—seems that the neighbors called in the police. There was some sort of a disturbance."

"Are my sons there?"

"I think you'd better talk to Talbot."

I went into the house with its beamed ceilings and white walls and ancient oak furniture, and in the shadowy hall I paused and looked into the oak-paneled study where the police surgeon was examining Sir James's body. There was a phone on the desk but I didn't want to intrude so I went up the stairs to an extension phone in the hall outside Liz's bedroom.

A police sergeant answered and called Talbot. I could hear people shouting in the background. Or laughing. Or screaming.

"What the hell's going on there?" I yelled at Talbot who could hardly hear me above the ruckus.

"I was hoping you'd be able to answer that. I think you'd better get up here. Your little writer's joke has gone far enough."

"Talbot, if you know a joke that would make me laugh

right now, tell me. Did you know we've had two murders down here, and my boys are still missing and my wife has just collapsed? I'm not in a mood to be patronized by Scotland Yard or anyone else."

"Calm down and explain to me what happened."

"What happened is that Sybil Rodne and Bunting have been murdered and Sir James has died of a heart attack and I can't explain any of it, and you're talking to me about jokes. For God's sake, what's all that noise?"

"Mr. Armacost, I can understand your feelings, and this may seem to be of rather secondary importance under the circumstances, but could you possibly tell me how a burial urn missing from Westminster Abbey came to be in your attic with a tape recorder running inside it? Listen . . ."

He held the phone away and I could hear the demoniacal laughter and howls echoing through the house.

I felt a cold hand grip my guts. The voices—I could swear they were Eddie's and Richard's. I felt dizzy with panic. "Talbot, are you sure that's a tape recorder?"

"What else could it be? The urn is too small for anyone to be hiding inside it. It looks to me as if your boys have played another one of their so-called pranks. How they ever got the bloody thing up there beats me. It must weigh three hundredweight."

"Then you haven't opened the urn? You haven't seen this tape recorder with your own eyes?"

"No, I'm not allowed to open the urn except in the presence of a Home Office official. We're trying to get a Home Office man to come here now. The urn is Crown Property and I can't touch it."

Suddenly the tone of his voice changed. He seemed to have remembered what I had been going through. "Anyhow this should put your mind to rest."

"About what, for Christ's sake?" The absurdity of the statement almost made me laugh.

"It should be obvious now that your boys' running away had nothing to do with the death of the school caretaker. They just wanted to be gone before the urn was discovered."

I didn't answer him. What was the point of trying to explain?

"Listen, I'm leaving right now and will drive up to London. I'll be there as soon as I can." I hung up before he could say any more and leaned my forehead against the cool plaster of the upstairs wall. I was remembering the shuffling noises I had heard in the attic of the house. And I prayed silently for the strength to take whatever was waiting for me there.

I turned away from the phone and opened the door of Liz's bedroom. She was sleeping soundly, her face relaxed. I closed the door quietly and went back down the stairs.

Devereaux was waiting for me as I came out of the house. "We've had to send for more dogs. I don't know what the hell is wrong with these two!"

"I do."

"What?"

"They were born five hundred years too late."

He looked at me strangely.

"Look," I said, "they want me in London. My wife is sleeping. I'll try to be back before morning." I left him staring at me and walked toward the car. Then I thought of something and turned around. "Inspector, do you have any idea what time those two in the barn were murdered?"

"The police surgeon says between four and five o'clock."

I nodded and got into the car. It had been four thirty exactly when Liz and I had noticed the writhing faces on the table as we left the house. I started the car and moved off down the gravel drive. An hour and a half to London. Eternity is ninety minutes long.

It was just past midnight when I reached home. The street on one side of the square had been blocked off and the flashing blue lights of police vehicles were everywhere. Crowds of people, some of them still in their nightclothes beneath hastily donned furs and overcoats, jammed the sidewalk and overflowed across the square itself. The noise was audible above the murmur of the crowd. Muffled, mocking, demoniacal laughter. It sounded strangely like the laughter of two small boys I had known a lifetime ago, twisted and parodied by demons.

I crossed the street as a bobby came to intercept me. I gave my name and he hustled me inside.

Police lined the downstairs hall. Someone escorted me up the stairs to the landing where two uniformed sergeants, hands pressed over their ears, stood at the bottom of a ladder staring up into the loft. There were lights in the loft. And people talking—shouting to be heard above the all-pervading, spine-chilling laughter that seemed to come from all over the house at once. I ran up the ladder and bumped heads with Talbot who was crawling on all fours beneath the slope of the rafters. Two more police held portable floodlights. Then I saw the urn. It was not very big, but it was carved from solid stone and must have weighed a quarter of a ton. Whoever—or *whatever*—had brought it up there, it could not have been easy. Or could it?

A distinguished-looking man with iron-gray hair, incongruous in evening dress now well-covered with dust, watched as a workman with a blowtorch melted the lead seal around the lid of the urn. He turned to look at me and Talbot introduced us, shouting above the din, "Sir Geoffrey Hamilton from the Home Office—Mr. Armacost."

We nodded briefly and turned to watch the melting lead drip from the seal beneath the lid of the urn. The laughter, rattling from the rafters, was a physical thing that beat the air about us. Even if I had not recognized some quality in the timbre of the voices behind the laughter it would still have been awesome. As it was, I knew that laughter all too well, but never had I heard it before as I heard it now. There was nothing of childish merriment, nothing of carefree innocence about it. This was the laughter of the damned.

The last ribbon of molten lead dripped from the seal. The workman turned off his blowtorch and nodded, gripping the lid of the urn on his side. One of the police put down his floodlight and got hold of the lid from the other side. They lifted together.

The laughter stopped.

In the sudden silence I was conscious of the grating of the stone lid as it moved, and from the street below I could hear the murmur of the crowd like waves on a distant shore.

The lid was lifted aside and we crowded together, peering in.

There were a few small bones, obviously human.

There was a small lead box like the one I had seen at Pinewood. Inside was a plastic flower, hideous, black green, almost shapeless.

There were two smiling cherubic faces. From the hall table.

"Most extraordinary!" said Sir Geoffrey Hamilton.

"That seal has not been touched since the urn was replaced in the Abbey in 1933. And those things certainly weren't in there then."

Talbot looked at me. "Any suggestions?"

"Inspector, if I could explain all this—I could solve the riddle of the universe." I turned and went down the ladder, my legs trembling.

I hated to face the curious gawking crowd outside but I had to get out of the house. It was pressing down on me with all its weight. I walked by the table without really seeing it, went down the steps into the cold midnight air, and crossed to the car, pushing my way through the crush of people.

"Mr. Armacost!"

I turned to see Sergeant Digby clearing a way through the crowd as though moving something in front of him. Then I caught sight of a tousled head and my heart leaped. Was it . . . ? My God, yes it was! Richard. And Eddie. I shoved my way toward them, went down on my knees, and hugged them to me. I was crying.

The boys looked wan, bewildered, as if they had just been awakened from a dream. I looked up at Digby, oblivious of the now silent crowd staring at this strange spectacle of a grown man on his knees crying and hugging two dirty little boys. "Where did you find them?"

He pointed across the square. "A lorry driver dropped them off. Said he picked them up near Romsey. I've got his details—we'll question him later."

"Eddie . . . Richard!" I shook them, laughing, sniffling back the tears. "Where the devil have you been?"

Richard looked at Eddie, then back at me. "We don't remember," he said quietly.

Digby gave me a sympathetic glance. "They've been

through a lot, sir, from the look of them. If I were you I'd take them inside."

I nodded and got to my feet. They were really too big to carry but I picked them up, one under each arm, and staggered through the crowd and up the steps.

Sir Geoffrey Hamilton was in the hall, dusting his soiled evening clothes and talking to Talbot. Both turned when they saw me. Their impulse was to ask questions, but the boys were in no shape to answer.

Sir Geoffrey Hamilton was staring at the boys. "Mr. Armacost, do you mind if I have a closer look at these two lads of yours?" He saw my hesitant look and smiled. "It's quite all right, I am a doctor. Matter of fact I'm Home Office pathologist. These boys exhibit all the outward signs of emotional and physical exhaustion and I think it might be a good idea for me to examine them—if you don't mind."

Sir Geoffrey took the boys gently by the shoulders. "Come on, you two, into the front room and let's have a look at you!"

I started to follow but he stopped me. "Under the circumstances, Mr. Armacost, I'd like to conduct at least the first part of this examination with no one around. A parental presence might cause them to color their answers. You do understand?"

I nodded, but I didn't really. Still, I was glad to have a doctor look at them. And a very capable one, too, from the sound of things.

I went into the kitchen and made coffee and sat exchanging small talk with Talbot until the living room door opened about twenty minutes later and Sir Geoffrey beckoned to me. The boys passed me, going toward the kitchen. "Are there any cornflakes, Dad?"

"I—I don't know."

"Come on, you two," Talbot called amiably, "we'll find something to eat."

"Inspector!" Sir Geoffrey's note held a warning note. "No questions, understand? That's official."

Talbot nodded.

My talk with Sir Geoffrey was very brief. "Frankly, Mr. Armacost," he said as he repacked his bag, "I'm completely baffled. Some of the things your lads told me were beyond belief. I'd say they have been hallucinating. And their pulse rate and blood pressure are very low, abnormally so. Have they been under sedation?"

"They may have been," I said guardedly.

"You are referring to this Mrs. Rodne they mentioned, I take it?"

"Yes."

"I'd like to have a talk with that lady."

"I'm afraid that's impossible. She was butchered to death in the New Forest this afternoon by—I believe the correct term is, 'persons unknown.' "

He looked at me thoughtfully for a moment, then nodded, snapping shut his bag. "I see. Then I think we shall leave it at that." He offered me a cigarette and lit one for himself, exhaling smoke in a long, slow sigh. "I won't dwell on what they said, Mr. Armacost. Matter of fact they didn't say much. Because they couldn't remember. Sort of drug-induced amnesia. But from what Talbot has told me previously I had pieced a few things together."

"Will they be—are they all right?" I held my breath.

"Perfectly. They're normal, healthy, and very intelligent young boys. Fortunately, the herbal drugs they apparently took were amnesiac. They will never recall a thing. Whatever happened will remain in this room. I will not discuss it with Inspector Talbot. Even if I did, I doubt he would believe me. Let's just say that what little they told me is the strangest thing I've encountered in a long and checkered medical career. I doubt we shall ever really know what happened."

"My only worry is about the boys."

"Then put your mind at rest. They are now perfectly normal."

He picked up his bag and turned at the door to shake my hand warmly. "Thank you, Mr. Armacost."

"What on earth for?"

"Thanks to you and your boys I've been spared sitting through a bloody boring after-dinner speech on the prevalance of liver fluke in moorland sheep."

He laughed and went out into the night.

I went into the hall and found the boys standing by the table. "Gee, Dad, I never realized it was such an *ugly* thing," Eddie said.

"Yeah," Richard chimed in. "Maybe we could sell it and get our money back, huh? Do you think Mom would mind?"

"I don't think so. Besides, I think it owes us something."

We crossed the square, now nearly empty of onlookers, and got into the car for the drive back to Hampshire. Within five minutes they were sound asleep in the back seat.

HISTORICAL NOTE

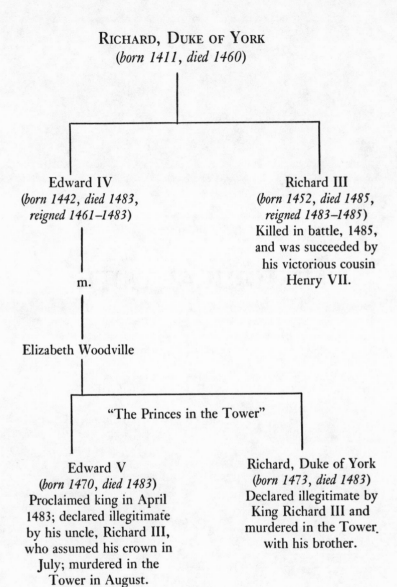

RICHARD, DUKE OF YORK
(*born 1411, died 1460*)

Edward IV
(*born 1442, died 1483,
reigned 1461–1483*)

Richard III
(*born 1452, died 1485,
reigned 1483–1485*)
Killed in battle, 1485,
and was succeeded by
his victorious cousin
Henry VII.

m.

Elizabeth Woodville

"The Princes in the Tower"

Edward V
(*born 1470, died 1483*)
Proclaimed king in April
1483; declared illegitimate
by his uncle, Richard III,
who assumed his crown in
July; murdered in the
Tower in August.

Richard, Duke of York
(*born 1473, died 1483*)
Declared illegitimate by
King Richard III and
murdered in the Tower
with his brother.

On Wednesday, April 9, 1493, King Edward IV of England died and was succeeded by his twelve-year-old son, Edward V. The boy's reign lasted approximately four months before he was brutally murdered, along with his younger brother, Richard, Duke of York, by Miles Forest and John Dighton at the orders of their uncle, King Richard III.

According to the "official" history by Sir Thomas More, King Richard dispatched a messenger named John Green to Sir Robert Brackenbury, constable of the Tower, ordering him to murder the two innocent princes. Brackenbury refused, and the King then sent Sir James Tyrell to London with a warrant to Brackenbury to deliver the keys of the Tower for one night. Tyrell, in turn, passed the keys to his groom, John Dighton, who, with the help of Miles Forest, one of four jailers in charge of the young princes, gained entrance to the sleeping princes' cell. Forest and Dighton smothered them with pillows, and, after calling Sir James to view the bodies, buried them at the foot of a staircase.

It was not until 1674 that actual proof was uncovered indicating where the princes were buried. Ten feet below the foundation of the original staircase in the White Tower, workmen discovered a wooden chest containing the skeletons of two children. The remains were identified as the princes' and were solemnly interred in Westminster Abbey, where they have remained peacefully for the past three hundred years.